PAJe 09/12

D0335721

This book should be returned/renewed by the
latest date shown above. Overdue items incur
charges which prevent self-service renewals.
Please contact the library.

Wandsworth Libraries
24 hour Renewal Hotline
01159 293388
www.wandsworth.gov.uk

Wandsworth

This book is dedicated to families.
The families we are born into,
the families we find, and the families we make.
Om Shanti.

JANETTA OTTER-BARRY BOOKS

Om Shanti Babe copyright © Frances Lincoln 2012
Text copyright © Helen Limon 2012
The right of Helen Limon to be identified as the author of this work

A catalogue record for this book is available from the British Library.

ISBN 978-1-84780-357-3

Set in Palatino

Printed and bound by CPI Group (UK) Ltd, Croydon, CR0 4YY

1 3 5 7 9 8 6 4 2

Om Shanti, BABE

Helen Limon

F

FRANCES LINCOLN
CHILDREN'S BOOKS

The Green Goddess

I woke up with sweaty pits and hamster-cage mouth. Five thousand miles on a plane and three dinners in one day but, as a look in my wash-bag showed, no toothbrush!

Running my tongue over furry teeth, I found a trail of crusty drool in the corner of my mouth. I groaned and rubbed my eyes, remembering, *waaaay* too late, the triple-thick mascara I'd applied back home. Uber-cool Cass arrives in style. Did this happen to people in first class, I wondered? Maybe they had special cabin crew to tidy them up while they slept. Or maybe rich people just didn't drool.

I unpeeled a curl of hair from my sticky cheek and tried to see through the curtain dividing us from the free champagne and goody bags. I'd begged Lula to go for the upgrade, but she'd gone *blah blah blah* about it being bad enough needing two tickets.

A TV screen embedded in the seat-back showed

a red arrow tracing a path from London and nudging land at our final destination. The cabin crew were starting to pack up the duty-frees and I was running out of time to get to the toilet. I wasn't sure I could even make it past my snoring neighbour, whose body spilled over the seat like a vanilla muffin.

A pointy elbow war had broken out at take-off, with our arm rest as the front line. Around Dubai I had called – apparently very convincingly – for a sick bag, and he'd moved pretty fast for a big bloke.

During all the fuss, Lula had woken up and shot me a Level Three death-stare. Her range ran from one to seven, starting with thin-lips-furrowed-brow and ending at total-face-freeze. She was asleep now. I watched her lips move and wondered what she was dreaming about.

She turned her head towards me and yawned. 'Nearly there, Cass. Are you excited?'

'Just a bit!'

'You know Bollywood isn't proper India, don't you?'

'Yeah… I bet it's pretty close though!'

I'd been practising dance routines over Christmas until Lula threatened to cancel our film club membership. How she expected me to learn anything about India was a mystery.

Lula sighed, then peered at me over her glasses. 'Are your eyes meant to look like that?'

'Like what?'

She passed me a packet of tissues from the pocket in the back of her seat. I squeezed passed Mr Snoozy and joined the toilet queue.

After I'd rinsed out my mouth, I sat for a while staring into the dull glow of the mirror. My mum was right, my face was a car crash. I'd tried to get the Bollywood Diva look, but my stubby eyelashes and frizzy hair just wouldn't play. I scrubbed off the mascara and splashed lots of cold water about.

I looked in the mirror again – even more tragic. It wasn't fair. I knew from the movies that all the girls in India would be really pretty, with long dark hair and huge eyes. How was I ever going to fit in? The seatbelt signs flashed and a grumpy air hostess harassed me back to my seat.

As we came in to land, Lula patted my shoulder and pointed out of the window. Below us were fishing boats painted in bright colours, their nets stretched out across the water behind them. On the river bank, flat-roofed houses sat neatly bunched together between the fields. An early-morning light was just touching the tips of the palm trees, turning them pink and gold.

Lula used this combination of colours in loads of her fabric designs. She called it Kerala Dawn and usually it sold by the truckload. Lula's shop was named after me, Cassia. Lula said we started, like the cassia tree, as a tiny idea that just kept growing.

Everything she stocked was from southern India, Kerala to be specific, all free-range and nicey-nicey. My mum was kind of a fair-trade freak, but the shop was super-successful and we even had a few celebrity clients.

Just before Christmas, Cassia was featured in a magazine under the headline, *Shops to Change the World*, but I don't think the world noticed and now we were having our biggest-ever January sale. It was weird having the shop so quiet. Lula rearranged the shelves a million times and ranted to Auntie Doré about cheap stuff from sweat-shop factories being unfair competition.

Yes, she'd definitely got a bit crazed without some winter sun, so the spring buying trip was brought forward. And guess what? This time I was tagging along too. School? Well, that was another story.

It took forever to get through Customs, and by the time we'd dragged our battered bags to the exit I was ready to shriek. I was in India to get sunshine and glamorama, and all the stupid forms and waiting for our cases was getting in the way!

The doors opened at last and warm air gushed in like a sauna. A mix of hot earth and incense sticks curled up my nose, and a row of ancient buses parked beside the exit doors added exhaust fumes to the fragrant mix. There were about a zillion people milling about too. Most of them were on their phones and the noise was unbelievable.

Lula snapped on sunglasses and launched herself into the crush. She seemed to have special crowd-negotiating powers, but I kept bumping into people and 'Sorry!' became a sort of dreary chant.

I was waiting to cross the road when an old man tripped over my bag and muttered something unfriendly-sounding under his breath. His thin legs poked out from the baggy sort-of-shorts he wore. I tried to think nice thoughts, because he was old, but it was pretty gross. My case had left a scratch and a little blood was trickling slowly over his knee.

I looked around for Lula. She was way ahead of me now and slowly disappearing into the crowd. I shouted another 'Oops, sorry!' to the old man and then ran after her, yelling 'Excuse me!' at random until I caught up.

Lula was waving at someone and, through the crowd, I spotted an emerald-coloured car I recognised from her photos. It was the Green Goddess, but it looked smaller and more old-fashioned in real life. An Indian man was making his way through the crowd towards us.

'Cassia, I want to introduce you to my friend, Vikram Chaudhury.'

The man smiled and reached out for my bag. His hand was cool and smelled of sandalwood. '*Namaste, Namaste*. Welcome, Cassia, and welcome back to Kerala, Luella. I trust you had pleasant flight?'

Lula experimented with a bit of banter in Malayalam and he only winced once so I thought she must be doing OK. She went to evening classes, and in the weeks leading up to a buying trip she chattered her way through repeat-after-me tapes while she made dinner.

Mr Chaudhury had been escorting Lula around for about three years now. She said he acted as guide, and finder of misplaced stuff. Even in London, Lula left a trail of purses, glasses and keys behind her.

Mr Chaudhury was leading the way back to the car. Lula walked close beside him, deep in conversation. They looked strange together. He was about the same age as her, plumper and not so tall. He wasn't wearing proper Indian clothes and his short-sleeved shirt was a brighter pink than even Dad would have dared buy. I hurried to catch up with them and linked my arm through Lula's.

We stowed our bags in the boot and inched out of the crowded car park, horn blaring. Lula sat in the front, so I had the whole back seat to myself. I stretched out my legs and wriggled my toes. Eau de stink-foot lurked around my sweaty shoes. I wondered if Indian girls got smelly feet. Probably not.

Everything went fast-forward when we joined the highway, and the traffic noise went up a couple of levels too. The road was lined with giant adverts for business schools, new apartments and women loaded down with gold wedding jewellery.

A girl pulled up alongside us on a moped.

Her helmet was painted with the Indian flag. It matched her outfit. I watched her steer past the front of the car, then she swerved out to avoid a massive pothole in the road. The Green Goddess braked hard. I slid forward in my seat and so did Lula. Her eyes were shut tight behind the giant sunglasses.

Mr Chaudhury patted her hand. It was his bad driving that threw us around so I was surprised when Lula didn't say anything. She didn't even push his hand away.

'Relax, ladies. You will be pleased to note that January is road-safety month in Kerala.' I could hardly hear him through the blaring of horns and squealing of brakes.

Lula pointed to a sign by the road that urged us to 'AVOID RASH DRIVING'. Not a chance! Looking around, the only way to do that would be to stay in the airport. Moped-girl sped off and we rejoined the random madness of Ernakulam in rush-hour.

The traffic got worse as we got closer to town but Mr Chaudhury never shouted or got stressed-out. Maybe the little stone elephant sitting on the dashboard kept him calm. Or perhaps it was the St Christopher stuck on to the steering wheel. Lula had one just like it, tied to her bicycle basket.

Lula got a bottle of water out of her bag and passed it over to me. 'It's snowing back home, Cass. I bet your school-friends wish they were here with you!'

'Yeah, I bet they do,' I replied. But I didn't really mean it.

'Year Ten is hard work. I hope they'll take class notes for you.'

'Yeah, me too,' I replied. But I didn't mean that either.

'Maybe you could find some nice postcards to send them?'

I opened the window a bit wider and fiddled with the seat-belt. The buckle was hot to the touch and the webbing rubbed against my neck. I took my iPod out of my bag. The battery was flat.

'Are you feeling OK, Cass?' Lula was using her *Idiot's Guide to Teens* voice.

I ran my tongue over my disgusting teeth. 'Have you got any mints?'

Lula rummaged around in her bag. 'No, sorry. Drink some more water.'

'It's not cold enough,' I said, dropping the bottle on the floor.

When I saw Mr Chaudhury frowning in the rear-view mirror I looked away. Why was he looking at me like that? It was kind of rude for him to keep staring at Lula, too. Why didn't he just concentrate on driving? That was his job, after all.

Cinnamon Toast
with a Slide-glide

The heat got fiercer, and my jeans were clinging like the skin on hot milk by the time the car stopped outside our guest house. I slid my feet back into squelchy shoes and looked through a pair of metal gates at the house. The building was three storeys high and white like toothpaste. Swirly trellising around the balconies reminded me of paper doilies at an old ladies' tea room.

Mr Chaudhury lifted our bags out of the boot and pushed open the gates. A smiley lady in a dark-green saree came hurrying out of the house and hugged Lula. I guessed she must be Mr Chaudhury's wife.

'*Namaste! Namaste!* Luella, my dear, it is so so good to see you again.' She turned to me and clapped her hands. 'This must be little Cassia about whom we have heard so very, very much!' She shooed Mr Chaudhury back to the car, then stood back and studied me. She was so keen to see my sweaty face and terminally frizzy hair that she put her glasses on. I felt like an ornament on Lula's super-discount shelf. 'Actually, not so little, I see. She is like you, Luella, but with much of her father too, I think.'

I looked at my sandals. Dust had settled into the spaces between my toes, outlining them in dark brown like a little kid's drawing. I wondered what Lula had told her about Dad. Probably nothing very good, but that wasn't fair – it wasn't his fault he was different.

For ages I had dreams that he'd come back and live with us again. I hoped that he'd change his mind and realise we loved him more than anyone else ever could. Sometimes, when he had a newspaper deadline to meet, he used to yell about the noise I made, and for the first few weeks I thought him going was my fault.

The day he left, I put my cd player in the cupboard under the stairs. Lula found it one day and told me the reason Dad had gone. Then she turned the music up loud, and we cried and ate a tub of ice-cream together.

'Don't be shy. All good dishes need a mixture of ingredients,' Mrs Chaudhury said, flipping her saree shawl over her shoulder. 'Please come, Cassia, I will show you where you are sleeping.' She slipped off her shoes and opened the front door.

I picked up my bag and followed her inside. The house was cool and the smell of jasmine and sandalwood drifted along the hallway.

Mrs Chaudhury's bare feet made a soft slapping sound as she walked. Her toenails were painted dark red. Maybe I should have taken off my shoes too?

I pictured my swollen feet leaving a line of sweaty prints on the polished wooden floor and clenched my toes. I wondered how she would feel about her husband flirting with Lula. Maybe they didn't mind that sort of thing in India.

Lula and I were sharing a room up on the top floor, with doors that opened on to a flat roof. Tubs of tomatoes lined the edge. I stepped through the fly-screen doors and looked out across the garden. Paper lanterns hung from the branches of a tree, like origami fruit, and from the lawn below I heard the hiss of a water sprinkler.

On the ground-floor terrace I could see

Mrs Chaudhury carrying glasses and a tall jug. Mr Chaudhury and Lula had their heads together over the shop order book: the order book I was supposed to be looking after. Lula was even letting him make notes on the pages.

I went back inside and tugged at the doors. The wooden frame stuck and they closed with a bang. Inside the bedroom a ceiling fan turned, gently moving the warm air around just enough to make it breathable. I slid out of my shoes and put my bag on the bed nearest the door. The mosquito nets were a glamorous touch, but I'd expected our room to be a bit more five-star-and-mini-bar. Dad wouldn't have rated it at all.

I cranked up the ceiling fan and, as the blades began to turn faster, something moved on the wall. A pale-pink lizard had scuttled along and stopped just inches away from the light switch. It blinked. A tiny tongue shot out of its mouth and slid back between its jaws. I stood very still, holding my breath.

The lizard blinked again as I moved slowly away from the wall and ran for the door. Lula would have a fit when I told her and, while Mr Chaudhury got rid of it, I would be able to reclaim the order book. But when I got downstairs no one seemed bothered about mini-beasts stalking the walls.

'They are called geckos, Cassia. We think of them as our guests. They will help keep your room free of spiders and flies,' Mr Chaudhury said. His teeth were very white and when he smiled, his mouth crinkled at the corners. What a creep. He'd made it sound like geckos were his best friends and that I was some kind of teen psycho-killer.

Lula looked a bit embarrassed. She had told me loads about India but, clearly, there were some things she'd left out.

When I got back to our room the lizard was in exactly the same place on the wall. As I watched, a fly crawled slowly past it. 'Well, go on then, get busy!' I muttered as I undressed.

I washed my hair and stayed under the cool water until my feet wrinkled. Then I brushed my teeth, slid into holiday shorts and was ready to hit the streets.

Lula and the Chaudhurys were eating by the time I got back downstairs. The food smelled of lime and coconut. I wanted us to make a quick exit, but Lula called out from the terrace, 'Come and have some food, Cassie. Vikram is a great cook – it's utterly delicious!'

'I'm not really hungry yet,' I lied.

'Are you going exploring already?'

'Yeah, I need some exercise.'

I thought Lula would come with me, but it was Mr Chaudhury who stood up. 'Perhaps I should escort you, Cassia?'

'That's kind of you, Vikram,' said Lula, as she piled more food on to her plate.

'It's OK, I like being by myself. Anyway, I've already got a guidebook.'

Lula frowned. 'Well, if you're sure. Stick to the main road and don't be long! You could get a couple of tubes of mosquito repellent while you're out.' She took a bundle of rupees out of her bag. 'Perhaps a long skirt would be better for sightseeing, Cass?'

'Sorry! No time to change now.' I pocketed the money and headed quickly for the gate.

As it clanged shut behind me, Mrs Chaudhury said something to Lula. I stopped to listen some more, but their voices were muffled by the hedge. This wasn't *exactly* how I had pictured our first shopping trip. The pavement outside the gate was all broken up and I kicked a stone hard into the scrubby grass.

The road from the guest house followed the boundary of a dusty playing-field. Tall trees lined the edges and a yellow dog lay panting in the shadows. In the centre, a game of cricket was starting. I stood and watched for a while. The dog wandered towards me. I went to stroke its head, but saw its back was covered in stinky red scabs and changed my mind. Grosserama! Why hadn't someone called the RSPCA?

I followed the map in the guidebook to the main shopping area and wandered up and down the high street for a while, buying postcards and browsing the gift shops. Most of them had radios going and I practised a few dance moves while I shopped. A couple of local people watched me. I added a bit of swagger to my *running-man* and finished with *slide-glide*. They probably hadn't seen proper street dance before.

I hadn't walked far, but my belly was making whale noises. The guidebook said there was a popular café just round the corner and, following the map, I shimmied down the next side street.

The breakfast menu was written out on a chalk board by the door, in English, thank goodness.

Fruit and cinnamon toast sounded just about perfect and I went inside. I stopped and stared at a painting titled Little Red Riding Hood that hung near the entrance. Miss Hood wore a saree with a bright red cloth draped over her head. A white tiger was lurking in the shadow of a palm grove, but she hadn't noticed.

Magazines and copies of the Hindu Times were scattered about the crowded tables. I sat down and gave the waiter my order. Everyone around me was busy eating so I checked my purchases while I waited for breakfast. I was a big postcard fan.

I started the first one without thinking. 'Rachie, babe! Inja hot but not very B'wood yet... I think our driver has a crush on Loopy Lu aaargh!!! He's married though so I guess she's safe...xoxo'

I turned the card over and looked at the picture. I'd found some especially gruesome images of a Goddess waving a sword and a severed head. She was called Kali and she had four arms. She looked pretty angry about something. I imagined Rachel's face cracking into a smile when the card arrived. The old Rachel. The new Rachel would do something else entirely.

I sat and chewed on my nails for a bit, then tore

the card into little pieces. The waiter came back with my food and I brushed the pieces on to the floor.

The plate was stacked high and chunks of papaya sat in a pool of honey.

'Enjoy,' said the waiter.

I got my head down for a serious calorie-fest and ate until my jaw actually hurt. Swallowing down the last of a pineapple smoothie, I let out a sigh of pleasure, leaned back in the chair and closed my eyes. Conversations from the surrounding tables murmured soothingly in my head. I was seriously sleep-deprived and must have drifted off for a minute or two, as my head banging against the back wall woke me with a start. Some little kids at the next table looked away, giggling. I did a quick spittle check, but my chin was clear.

The café was hitting rush hour and a line of people stood waiting. A group of local girls crowded round a mobile phone. They were laughing at a message or maybe it was a photo. Seeing me stand up, they hurried over and grabbed the empty seats. I heard them use a few English works mixed up with stuff I couldn't understand. I guessed they learned English at school. I wondered if they'd like to practise. I could be their new British Best Friend.

The waiter came to take their order. He cleared away my plate and I wished I hadn't troughed my food down so fast. I smiled and tried a *'Namaste'* to the girls, but I guess they didn't hear me. They were exactly how I imagined they would be – really pretty with straight, dark hair and huge eyes. God, how lame I was! Of course they didn't want to talk to me. I picked up my bag and left. They probably already had all the friends they needed.

Death-stare Deluxe

Just past the post office, I saw a shop with a painted wooden sign, *Stop 'n' Save,* hanging over the door. Bundles of plastic shopping bags dangled from hooks outside. The counter ran across the full length of the shop and lots of the stock was piled in boxes behind it. Sacks of rice, beans and nuts sat on the floor.

There were no prices on anything and the displays looked a bit random. I thought Lula would have been very *tsky-tsky* if she'd seen it. But she was probably still heads-together with Mr Chaudhury.

There seemed to be a special queuing system going on and I missed my turn a few times. Then, when it was only me left in the shop, I asked for Jungle Juice, a brand of mosquito cream I remembered seeing in the chemist at home.

The man behind the counter looked confused and pointed to a crate of soft drinks. I tried again, carefully saying each word quite loudly.

An old lady came into the shop and stood beside me. She said something quietly to the man. He shrugged and stared at my legs.

I made a buzzing sound and pointed to an imaginary mosquito hovering over my arm. My finger followed its flight then stabbed me on the elbow. The old lady coughed and dabbed her eyes with her saree. The man just carried on staring.

It was very hot in the shop and the shiny cover of the guidebook was slippery in my hands. I opened it and tried to find the word for mosquito cream. I heard the old lady's bracelets jingling as she lifted her shopping bags impatiently from one arm to the other. I was having a bit of trouble breathing. The man was still staring down at my legs and then, just as I was about to cave, I saw the bit about malaria in the guidebook and shouted it out.

'Ah! *Odomos!*' the man and the old lady said at the same time.

'Yes! *Odomos!* Can I buy two bottles, please?'

'Yes, yes, but not from here. This is the wrong sort of shop. You must be in a different shop for such things. Goodbye.'

The old lady stepped forward quickly to take her turn and I staggered out. I felt a bit stupid, but why didn't they just sell the sort of stuff that visitors really needed?

Directly opposite was the entrance to a funky-looking bookstore. A *Harry Potter* was in the window and I stepped inside. Comics piled on a shelf rustled gently, their pages rising and falling as a ceiling fan stirred the air.

A woman behind the counter glanced up from the till and said, '*Namaste*.' Her hair was plaited and she had a red dot between her eyes.

I said '*Namaste*' back, putting the palms of my hands together to copy the little bow thing she'd done.

It took a few minutes for my eyes to forget the bright sunshine outside and, until I could see properly again, I just ran my fingers along the book spines. The shelves were tightly packed, loaded with cookbooks, yoga manuals, travel guides and second-hand novels that tourists had traded in. I picked through other people's reading, feeling like a spy. Someone had made notes in *One Night at the Call Centre* – a total double-digit-death-stare offence, yes indeed!

'You might like this.' A girl sorting books in the next row was holding up a paperback, *The Peacock Spring* by Rumer Godden.

'What's the story?'

'Actually, it's about a British girl who comes to India and gets herself into all sorts of trouble.'

'Is it funny?'

'No! Not at all!'

'Does it have a happy ending?'

She didn't answer straight away, which wasn't a good sign. 'In a manner of speaking… the girl, Una, goes back to school and actually that is what she really wanted all the time.'

'Sounds perfect,' I said, but I didn't mean it. How could going back to school ever be a happy ending? I read the blurb on the back. It sounded like she was in for a hard time. 'Thanks.'

'You are most welcome. This copy is trade-in, so it is with discount too.' With a smile, she handed me the book and went back to alphabetising the shelves.

I couldn't put it back, but when she wasn't looking I grabbed something from the fast cars and random explosions section as well, checking out the cover which showed a man on a jet-ski, waving a big gun.

The lady at the till watched as I sorted out Lula's rupees, and then gave me my change. She dropped the books into a cloth bag with the name of the shop printed on in thick ink.

'Excuse me, do you know where I can buy some *Odomos*, please?'

'Yes, there is a chemist shop nearby. Mosquito cream is very sensible, though keeping covered up will help greatly, you know.' She pointed over the counter at my legs.

What was these people's problem with skin? Even Loopy Lu was on my case. It seemed like now we'd arrived she was acting even more mentalist than usual. Maybe Mr Chaudhury was a bad influence.

No one was about when I got back to the guest house. I changed into long trousers and wandered round the garden for a bit, hoping Lula would appear.

Why had she gone off without me and where had she gone, anyway? I wanted to give her the *Odomos* and tell her all about breakfast and the bookshop. There was no sign of Mr Chaudhury either. The lawn sprinkler was still turning and I let jets of cool water run over my grubby feet.

Mrs Chaudhury waved at me through the kitchen window and said that Lula would be back very, very soon and that I should rest before lunch. She passed me an icy glass of soda.

I went upstairs, took a pile of cushions off the beds and sat out on the roof, sipping my drink. It was a mixture of lime and ginger. I really wanted a Coke, but in a weird way the spicy taste sort of suited the view.

I read the blurb on the back cover of *The Peacock Spring* again. It looked interesting, but I wasn't in the mood for a proper girl story and I cracked the spine on Mr Jet-ski instead. He didn't let me down, the body count hitting double figures well before the pages did.

As I finished my drink, I heard someone talking on the downstairs terrace. I leaned over to see if it was Lula back again. I couldn't see very well through the leaves, but her voice carried up to the roof.

'I hope she's OK... nothing serious, anyway.'

I guessed she was talking about me and I ducked back behind the plants.

A man's voice came in reply. 'It is all probably just storm in a teacup.' It sounded like Mr Chaudhury.

'She's been moping around the shop for weeks.'

'We will keep her busy.'

'I expect the sunshine will do her good, too.'

'And what about you, Luella? You have enough

on your plate without dramas cooked up by teenage girls.'

'This trip would be easier if she'd stayed in London. I just wish she was happy at school.'

'Happy or unhappy, the sooner Cassia is back pursuing her education the better.' His words flew through the bunches of green tomatoes and landed with a slap.

Without thinking, I picked up the book I'd been reading and threw it into the garden as hard as I could. My lips felt trembly and I took a couple of deep breaths.

What did my mum mean and why were they talking about me? Our life was none of Mr Chaudhury's stupid business. This was supposed to be *our* time together, just me and Lula. I was supposed to look after the order book and help her with the shop business, not him.

I wasn't going back to school. I was going to work in the shop with Lula for ever, and nosy Mr Chaudhury wasn't going to get in between us.

Kiss-kiss-cry-cry

The next morning I found Lula sitting on the terrace, eating breakfast. As I sat down at the table, she looked up from the paper she was reading.

'Morning, slumber-beast, have some food.'

'Not hungry.'

'Please, have something.'

'Can we go swimming today?'

'There isn't a beach nearby, Cass.'

'I was reading about this place in the guidebook, Serenity Spa, on Bolghatty Island. It sounds super-swishy.'

'I've been there before, it's super-expensive!'

'I could use some of Dad's Christmas money.'

'Sorry, Cassie, I hate playing tourist when I'm here. Besides, I've got an appointment at the bank this morning.'

'Can I come with you?'

Lula fiddled with one of her earrings, twisting

it round and round between her thumb and forefinger.

'How about, instead, I drop you at the spa?'

I took a piece of toast from under its anti-fly tent and peeled away the crusts. I dipped them one by one in a pot of honey. Normally, Lula does death-stare deluxe when I do this, but today she said nothing.

'Don't they have any cereal here?' I said, but she wasn't listening any more. She was reading the newspaper. 'Oh for goodness sake, some pop star is visiting and it's a bigger story than the fair-trade conference.'

'Who?'

'Jonny something… Jonny Gold.'

If sound had a colour, then the squealing noise I made was super-pink. Lula's eyebrows went shooting up her forehead.

'Hand over that paper right now!' I practically shrieked.

With a sigh, she tore out the page and flipped it across the table. There he was, my supercrush, Jonny Gold, tousled hair, dark eyes, little-boy-lost expression and a killer tattoo on his suntanned forearms.

The story had a bit about his new single, *Om Shanti, Babe,* but it seemed like the reporter was more interested in his "stunning (and now ex) film-star girlfriend" than in Jonny's music. He guessed Jonny was sulking somewhere Taj Mahalish – miaow!

My dad would have called this a *kiss-kiss-cry-cry* story. He was a proper journalist and spent half his life in a flak jacket and the other half going through people's bins. Lula called him 'the ink pig' when she thought I wasn't listening.

'Come on, Cass. If we're going to catch the ferry to Bolghatty we need to get our skates on.'

I carefully folded up the picture of Jonny Gold and slid it into my back pocket. 'Will it be OK to wear my bikini?'

'You'll be in tourist world, sweetie. I don't suppose anyone will mind.' The way she said it reminded me of going to nursery school in a fairy costume and clicky-clacky shoes. No one had minded that either, but I was just a little kid then.

Lula came with me as far as the reception desk, and said she would be back to pick me up at lunchtime. Aside from the staff, no one else was around and I felt a bit abandoned when she left. I mean, I was all by myself in a strange country. Dad would not have approved.

Lula hadn't said much on the boat-ride either,

and kept making notes in the order book. Losing this notebook was the one thing, aside from global poverty, that sent Lula into a complete, hysterical panic. It had a note taped on the front cover offering a big reward to finders in Malayalam, Hindi, Urdu, and about fifteen other languages including English.

In the back of the book were the names and addresses of her regular customers and she'd spent ages this year writing them all extra-special Christmas cards. Lula seemed super-stressy today, but I guessed it was just one too many breakfast coffees.

The pool was shaded by jungly creepers that scaled the walls around the courtyard and formed a green ceiling high above the water. I floated on my back, staring up at pink flowers dangling down like grow-your-own earrings. Through half-closed eyes, I watched tiny birds darting from flower to flower, their wings all blurry against the leaves.

A waterfall bubbled out of the wall and splashed on to the painted tiles lining the pool. Even the tables were inlaid with glass, and the whole place felt like a shrine to Saint Deluxury.

As I floated across the pool, I could hear the thud of my heart beating. It vibrated in my head, mixing with the gurgling sound of the water. Just then, I wondered what sound my soul would make – maybe a humming noise or something like a purring cat asleep in the sun.

There was a Jonny Gold song I loved that said your soul could travel no faster than a galloping horse, so when we zoom about it takes a while to catch up.

As I floated in the deep end, the noises around the pool muffled by the water in my ears, I imagined my soul somewhere near Mumbai heading south, a tiny firefly of pulsing pink light homing in on me from high in the sky. I wondered what happened if you kept moving so fast that your soul never found you again....

A shadow passed over the sun. I lost concentration and sank. Underwater, my normally uncooperative hair floated gently around like a shampoo advert and I held my breath for as long as I could. Would I still have friends if I had shampoo-advert hair?

I pictured myself swimming up to the surface and spotting my ex-best-friend Rachel sunbathing, poolside. I'd sneak up to her and shake cold water all over her back. She'd be a bit mad with me, but she wouldn't look at me like she hated me. Then we would order a big plate of chips and go for a swim and argue about what we would wear that night. We would talk about Jonny Gold, and dream about meeting him and getting back-stage passes and him thinking we were so cool and dedicating a song to us.

I surfaced with a gasp. It was time to get out. I kept my eyes closed as long as I could, but Rachel wasn't lying on a lounger. I was still all by myself. I ordered a cheese toastie and a Coke and started on my Peacock girl-in-trouble book.

It was weird reading about an English girl coming to India. It's not like we were similar or anything – Una, the heroine, was a big-brain, rich kid who wrote to her dad, Edward, in Latin for fun! Her mum was dead and she was not as pretty as her little sister, Hal. Plus her governess, Alix, was kind of mean because she was secretly sleeping with Una's dad and everyone disapproved, especially the servants, who thought she was not quite *Pukka*, whatever that meant. Everyone was keeping secrets and it was getting them all into trouble.

I finished my Coke and ordered an ice-cream. I was about to dip my spoon into a creamy mound of chocolate when a shadow fell across the table.

'I am very sorry, Cassia, but that is not a good idea.' It was Mr Chaudhury. He picked up the plate of ice-cream and gave it back to a passing waiter. 'Actually, I am of the opinion that ice-cream is best left to our American cousins. It is not really an Indian speciality and you do not want to get sick in your first week here, do you, m'n?'

I was so surprised that I dropped the spoon. It landed on the table with a clatter.

'Where's Mum?'

'Her meeting has gone on a bit. She said she is very sorry and I have come to collect you, instead.' He was smiling at me and his smile was wide and friendly, but I felt furious about my ice-cream.

'Pack up your things, Cassia. There is a ferry due soon and on the journey we can talk. It will be pleasant to get to know you a little better.'

But all I thought was, "I definitely don't want to get to know you, Mr Creepy-ice-cream-stealer, so why do you care about getting to know me?"

Boys' Own Fascinating Facts

We walked in silence to the ferry. Well, I walked in silence while Mr Please-call-me-Vikram did his tourist-guide thing. I sat in the women's section of the boat and, from the other side, he pointed out crummy old buildings that lined the banks.

When we landed, he launched into the history of Kochi. He did know loads about the place and I had to admit that some of it was interesting. But I was still annoyed about my lost ice-cream and stuck with giving him the silent treatment.

He had run out of *Boys' Own Fascinating Facts* by the time we reached the guest house, which was a relief. But to my complete horror, as we approached the gate I saw the jet-ski book lying on the step. I hadn't expected to see it ever again. Hopefully, Call-me-V would just think a tourist had dropped it or something.

He picked the book up, read the title and raised

his eyebrows.

'It just slipped out of my hands.'

'Do you wish to have it back?' He held the book out to me and we both stared at the mangled remains.

'No, thanks. I've got another one.'

'I can only pray that it is a little more worthy,' he sighed.

'Oh, there you are.' Lula had come through the gate and she looked tired. 'Move over, Cass, I've had a right cow of a day and I really need a shower.'

She marched straight past us and into the house. I noticed Call-me-V's surprised look and guessed he hadn't seen Lula in a stress-strop before. I followed her up the stairs and sat out on the roof, listening, as the water ran and ran. Lula hardly ever shouts. It's like the bad mood seeps out of her skin and she has to wash it down the plughole before she can be nice again.

I stared out across the empty garden. There was no one for me to talk to and nothing for me to do until Lula got out of the shower. I got a cushion off my bed and picked up the Peacock book.

Things were getting worse for Una and by a super-weird coincidence there was a character called Vikram in it now. He was an ex-prince who lived in a huge house and was in love with the wicked stepmother/governess, too. Alix, the governess, tried to ignore him and pretend nothing was happening, but everyone could see what was going on.

I felt sorry for Una, like she was a friend in trouble. But then I thought, if I had a real friend I wouldn't need a book one.

That evening I sat staring at a heap of clothes cascading out of my case. Lula had banned the shorts and anyway, even plastered in *Odomos*, being covered up would stop the mosquitoes gorging on my flesh like it came with extra fries. Jeans and a long-sleeved kaftan were at the top of the heap, so they would have to do.

We were having dinner at a local restaurant. Lula said the owner, Mr Rao, told you what was on the menu and that was that. I was a bit nervous about the food. Even though we sell Indian stuff, the shop keeps Lula too busy to cook properly in the evenings and we eat a lot of random ready meals. She used to get the organic ones, but lately it's been whatever's on the whoopsie counter.

Dad loves restaurants, the fancier the better, and he always books ahead. When we go for our Dad-Daughter bonding sessions he always treats me to a big dinner. The waiters seem surprised sometimes, when we arrive. Like they knew Dad's name, but they weren't expecting him to have a family.

He's really fierce about table manners and he drilled me about not using my left hand for eating in India. He even threatened to write *poo-paw* on it, to remind me why I shouldn't. He told me mathematical zero was invented in India, so I didn't see why toilet paper hadn't caught on yet.

Lula had a headache and decided we should walk the short distance through the streets. I was hoping her bad mood would keep Call-me-V out of the way for the evening or, even better, the rest of the trip. But no, there he was, smiling away as he guided us to the restaurant. He had got dressed up and he even looked sort of handsome. I thought Mrs Chaudhury must have been sad about being left behind and I was a bit disgusted that Lula didn't invite her, too.

On the way, I saw a lady sitting in the dust on the opposite side of the road. She didn't have proper fingers on her hands and she was holding the stumps out to the people passing by. I couldn't help staring at her even though it made me feel sad and a bit sick.

A man walked by her, talking on his mobile phone. I saw his gold watch catch the light as he tossed some money on the ground, but he didn't look at her. He didn't even stop talking on his phone.

The restaurant was full, but Lula saw some Indian business friends and we joined them at their table. I wanted to sit next to her, but her friends had brought their little kids along and so instead I became children's entertainer for the evening.

Over their chatter, I could just about hear Lula talking about threads per inch and shipping costs. I needed to learn about this stuff too, but it was too noisy in the restaurant to listen properly.

The waiter brought a mixture of dishes on a big platter. In the middle was some *naan* bread and a bowl of soupy lentil stew. The kids got stuck into the food straightaway, scooping chunks of coconut-scented fish on to the *naan* and topping it with a dollop of yoghurty stuff.

I was thinking about having a try when Lula said she was sorry there weren't any chips, but that if I wanted she would order an omelette or something for me instead. She said it quite loudly and the whole table stared at me. It was totally humiliating and my appetite instantly dried up with shame. Why didn't she just mash a baby banana and have done with it?

I just picked at the *naan* bread and watched the tinies demolish the chicken. They had a kind of milk smoothie thing for pudding and my impersonation of a walrus with drinking-straw tusks made them laugh themselves into exhaustion until they fell asleep in their chairs.

I watched to see if Lula had noticed me not eating, but she was getting deeply into work stuff. I tried to interrupt her and she looked a bit cross.

Then Call-me-V said there was an internet café nearby and why didn't I take a tuk-tuk and 'do some surfing' and Lula said 'what a good idea', and that she'd be along soon, and then she gave me another bundle of rupees.

Call-me-V stood up and said he would escort me there. Why couldn't he just mind his own business? I didn't want him trailing around after me, pointing out 'historical monuments from our colonial past' like some history teacher.

I said I had to go to the bathroom and when no one was looking I sneaked out of the side door. Lula probably wouldn't notice I'd gone, she was so busy being best buddies with Call-me-V and not taking any notice of me. Maybe she wouldn't even care.

Next thing I knew I was out in the night, by myself, trying to choose between a gang of auto-rickshaws.

One of the drivers dropped his cigarette butt into the dusty ground and walked towards me. 'Where are you going?'

'The internet café on Church road, please.'

'I know a better one, I will take you there, much better prices.' He pointed me towards his tuk-tuk. It was painted in swirls of neon and had a Ferrari sticker on the front. Lining the dashboard were plastic figures of Elvis Presley. Their hips jiggled and twinkled in the glare of the street lamps.

'My mum said I have to go to the one on Church Road.'

'My one is better, very popular with tourists, come!' He was standing right in front of me. I could smell cigarette smoke on his breath.

'It's OK, thank you. Maybe I should just walk.'

'It is very, very far to walk, you must please come with me.'

I looked back at the door of the restaurant. Light and loud voices spilled out on to the street. I wanted to go back inside, but I was too embarrassed to face everyone. If I couldn't even take a tuk-tuk by myself they'd think I was a real baby. I looked at the other drivers laughing together in the dark.

'Just take me to the internet café on Church Road, please.' I held out the bundle of rupees.

'Hey, stop hassling her, yah!' An arm reached out and pushed down my outstretched hand. I recognised the girl from the bookshop. She said something else to the driver. I didn't understand it, but she sounded pretty annoyed.

His friends were laughing at him now and he looked down at his feet until she'd stopped scolding. 'OK, OK, don't shoot! Please, please, lady, get in.'

The girl held my wrist and pulled me towards the tuk-tuk. 'Actually, I will ride with you, if that's OK?'

'That would be great, thanks.'

'What is your name?'

'Cassia, I'm from London.'

'So, how are you getting along with your book?'

I told her that Una had just met Ravi, the poet boy who lived in the garden, and that she was sneaking off to see him at night. I said I thought it was nice she had someone to talk to.

She shook her head and patted my hand. 'As a matter of fact it is going to get worse before it is getting better.'

There was a computer free at the internet café, so I bought a packet of crisps and settled down for an hour in the online world. Dad had already emailed with a reminder about washing my hands after you-know-what and not drinking the tap water. The man spent his life laughing at danger but where I was concerned…

I was impatient to catch up with the online gossip about Jonny Gold, so I did a quick reply to Dad making it sound like I was on intravenous boiled water and covered in a layer of sunscreen as thick as icing sugar. Trust my luck to get his hair and Lula's pale skin.

The news from Gilded Bear records was a real eye-popper. It seemed Jonny had flown from London to Bangalore to make a music video for *Om Shanti, Babe*. He said he 'wanted to be close to the spirituality that had inspired the new song'.

I was so surprised I actually said, 'OMIGOD!' out loud, which was practically a hanging offence in our house. Bangalore was almost up the road, in India terms, which meant I could actually be sharing air with the golden one. I'd been in supercrush mode over Jonny for nearly a year and just the thought of him made my hands shake so much I could hardly type straight.

I listened to the track online. The words were all about being chilled out and it had a sitar bit for the chorus, but it didn't sound as Indian as I expected.

I was still reading Jonny Gold's amazing song lyrics when I saw Lula waving at me from the doorway. There was no sign of Call-me-V and I logged off. I tried to tell her about Jonny Gold, but she was in mini-rage mode and I was too tired to make her listen.

She gave me a long boring lecture about not sneaking off, and how I'd offended Call-Me-V and embarrassed her in front of her business friends and *blah blah blah*. She was warming up for the dead-in-a-ditch speech when we got back to the guest house and I crawled into bed, pulling the sheet over my head.

I thought it would be nice sharing a room, but Lula was an angry million miles away. I warned her that the moment she started snoring I would take her credit card and demand my own room.

She just frowned and said, 'Good luck squeezing another penny out of that!' Then she said she had jet-lag and went back downstairs, leaving me by myself in the dark again. She obviously cared more about what Call-me-V was doing than me.

As I lay there, listening to the traffic noise and dogs barking, I wished I was back at home, cosy under my own duvet instead of sweating away in India, frizzy-haired and friendless.

In the middle of the night I got up for a drink of water. Lula still wasn't in bed and I sat by the window, looking out on to the garden. Shadows of two people danced on the lawn and I leaned out to take a better look. Through the branches of the lantern tree I saw Lula and Call-me-V. They were standing very close together, holding hands. Then he leaned forward and kissed her on the lips.

Karma Cookies

At stupid o'clock I woke up with my arms all tangled in netting. Itching feet told me that some little visitors had got through the layers of *Odomos* and bitten me. I scowled at the geckos lurking by the skirting board. I'd had a bad dream. I felt a knot in my stomach and rubbed my head.

Suddenly my dream came screeching back into my head. Only I knew it wasn't a dream. Lula and Call-me-V had been kissing in the garden in the middle of the night. I'd seen them with my own eyes.

I felt sick. It was just like the Peacock book, only Call-me-V wasn't Ravi, the handsome poet, he was our driver and Lula wasn't Una, she was my mum! Poor Mrs C! I just lay there, eyes shut, watching an action replay of the stomach-churning kiss over and over in my head until I thought I was going to heave.

'Five minutes, Yogi Bear!' Lula shouted from the bathroom. She was singing to herself. It was a happy sound, totally tuneless, but happy. How could she be happy?

I put my head back under the bed covers. Lula shouted again from the bathroom. She'd found a Yoga class and said it might be good for my dancing. But I didn't feel like dancing now, I felt like screaming. I dragged myself out of bed and hunted around for a clean T-shirt.

In the guidebook it said that Yoga was a really big deal here and there were lots of different styles to choose from. There was even one where you just stood around and laughed. I'd read that Yoga started over two thousand years ago and, if you practised it every day, it was supposed to make you feel 'at one with the divine'. They did it at our community centre and the ladies always looked quite cheerful coming out. As I pulled on my leggings, I thought it would take more than Yoga to make me feel cheerful.

We walked the short distance across town to the class. The streets were already busy with people hurrying along. Lula said the loudspeakers I could hear were calling people to pray in the mosques.

Small piles of burning rubbish were dotted along the pavement. A man was sweeping dry leaves on to the piles. It looked like the smoke was making his eyes hurt.

It was practically dawn, and I couldn't believe Lula didn't get a tuk-tuk. Where was Call-me-V? I thought he was supposed to be our driver. Then I realised he was probably still snoozing in bed with poor Mrs Chaudhury and I had to rub my eyes hard to get rid of that picture, too.

What was I going to do? Lula and Call-me-V couldn't get it together, could they? Mrs Chaudhury would die of a broken heart. What if he came and lived with us in London? Would he help Lula run the shop instead of me?

Maybe we should just fly back home now, before it was too late. I could pretend to be very very sick or something. Then I remembered school and realised I was trapped here in Kerala, with my mad irresponsible mother and her horrible cheating boyfriend.

Lula did her chatty-Cathy act all the way, but I was on silent mode. She looked a bit confused, but I figured that served her right.

We made our way to Mahatma Gandhi Road and found the school. It was in the downstairs of a building beside a convent. Painted in blue letters on the wall outside, it said, *Let us be happy to do what we can.* I imagined a hooded nun sneaking out in the night with a spray can and wondered what God would think. Incense drifted out of the front doors.

Inside it was clean and brightly lit but not nearly as glitzy as the Serenity Spa. Blue Yoga mats were laid out ready, and in the middle there was a small group of serious-looking people, standing completely still and breathing very loudly. Of course, I was the youngest person in the room. Where were all the teen yogis? Oh yes, probably still in bed!

My stomach gurgled and the teacher gave me an encouraging smile. 'This is a good sound. Your belly is waking up.'

'Yeah, waking up grumpy,' I muttered.

The lesson started with a long stretch the teacher called a Sun Salutation. It was quite easy and made me feel more awake. Then we did some twists and some standing on one leg. I couldn't keep my balance and hopped around the room for a bit until the teacher caught me. It started to get a lot harder after that and only a very bendy couple were left trying to tie themselves into pretzels. The effort was turning their faces purple.

Lula seemed to be enjoying it and the teacher kept telling her she was doing really well. Then she lost her balance and giggled when he caught her.

What was happening? First Mr Chaudhury and now a yogi! Was she always like this in India? It was a good thing I'd come along to keep an eye on her.

We got back to the guest house and I went straight upstairs for another shower. When I came down again, breakfast was laid out on the terrace. Mrs Chaudhury seemed a bit hurt when I turned down everything she'd cooked, but how could I eat her food when I knew what was really going on? Though a guilty conscience didn't stop Lula tucking in.

I groaned and laid my head flat on the table, on top of the order book.

'You OK, Cass?' Lula asked. 'I thought you might like to come to the market with me this morning.'

'I'm feeling a bit sick, actually.'

'Was it the Yoga?'

'Yeah, sort of…'

'Well, I have to go, I'm afraid. Would you mind if I left you behind?'

'I don't care; you always do whatever you want, anyway.'

Lula's coffee cup cracked back on to the saucer. She was staring at me. I knew I was being rude and at home she would have fired off a double-barrelled death-stare. It flashed for a moment, then Mrs

Chaudhury came in with more toast and she lowered the guns.

'You are very welcome to stay with me today, Cassia, if you like?' Mrs Chaudhury was smiling and I felt my face go red. 'We can do some cooking and maybe you would like a *mehandi*, m'n?'

I didn't know what a *mehandi* was, but before I could ask, Lula butted in. 'That sounds lovely, doesn't it, Cass? Say thank you to Lalitha.'

I couldn't believe how nicey-nicey she was being. What was she going to say when Mrs Chaudhury found out? 'Oops-a-daisy, I didn't think you'd mind if I lip-locked with your husband. Let's have a lovely cup of tea.'

Really… I mean… really!

After breakfast, Lula and Call-me-V set off in the Green Goddess and I helped Mrs Chaudhury's kitchen lady clear away the dishes. She made us both a glass of ginger soda, and me and Mrs Chaudhury sat at the table.

'Shall I open the shutters? Then we can have a nice view of the garden.'

The lantern tree cast a shadow on to the floor. I moved my chair, keeping my back to the open window.

'I think you are a little afraid of Indian dishes, Cassia, m'n?'

'I just don't like spicy things very much.'

'Actually, food here in Kerala is not so spicy-dicey. Shall we try to make something sweet, like coconut cookies?'

She fetched some storage jars from a cupboard and set them out on the table in front of me. As she measured the ingredients from each jar in turn, her gold bracelets jangled. They'd probably been a present from Call-me-V. They were so pretty, but she wouldn't want to wear them when she found out.

I remembered Lula putting her wedding ring away in a little box when she and Dad split, and I suddenly felt so sad I could hardly follow what Mrs Chaudhury was saying.

'This is *rava*, I believe you call it semolina. Next is sugar, then powdered cardamom, grated coconut, and last of all a little milk. Wash your hands and you can knead this into dough.'

I slid my fingers into the crumbly mixture, cupping my hands into scoops and pressing and folding it around until a soft lump formed. She showed me how to take chunks of the dough and roll it to make little balls. I licked my fingers. The mixture was sweet and smelled delicious. We squished the balls into patties and laid them in a pan on the stove. They sizzled as they hit the hot oil and I watched them bob about in a cushion of bubbles until they turned golden brown.

Whatever happened, Call-me-V would have to be a complete ejit to swap Mrs Chaudhury's cooking for Lula's.

'So, Cassia, while our morning treats are cooling down I shall give you a *mehandi*, a henna tattoo, and you can tell me all about London. I have never been and I am looking forward to seeing it.'

'Are you going on holiday?'

'I am hoping to see the Queen, and Vikram wants to visit your mother's shop, of course.'

My stomach gave a lurch. I looked up at Mrs Chaudhury. Did she suspect anything? She was so nice. How could Lula do this to her? Why didn't she find someone in London, someone like Dad? Well, not exactly like Dad – clearly that wasn't the answer.

Mrs Chaudhury was pointing at some photos from a magazine. The girl's hands were completely covered with lines and swirls traced out in orange dye. As I looked down at the pictures she gently stroked my fingers. 'I think this one would be very nice for you, you have such pretty hands. It is a pity you are biting your nails.'

She took a small cone-shaped package off the shelf behind her and snipped the pointed end with scissors. I was embarrassed when she lifted my sweaty hand on to her lap, but the silk felt cool and reassuring.

'Shall I put somebody's initials in the design?'

On a weird impulse I asked her to paint JG for Jonny Gold, surrounded by tiny stars, on to the inside of my wrist.

Smiling, she asked if that was my boyfriend's name and I said, 'Yeah, right, I wish!'

Mrs Chaudhury gave me a strange look and said, 'Be careful what you are wishing for, my dear,' in a deadly serious voice. 'Tell me, who is this Mister Jolly Gee you are thinking about?'

'He's an amazing singer in this band and he writes all the songs. He's really famous in England.'

'And why do you like him so very, very much?'

'Because he's really cool and he cares about stuff and when I listen to his music it's like he almost knows who I am. I mean, if I met him, I'm completely positive we'd get on really well straightaway.'

'He sounds like a dream, my dear, and sometimes that is how things should stay.'

'Mrs Chaudhury, have you and Mr Chaudhury got any children?'

'Me and Vikram with children?…No!' She looked astonished and then started to laugh. A fat drop of henna flew out of the packet and landed on my arm.

'Sorry, I didn't mean to be rude.'

'Cassia, I have a grown-up daughter, but Vikram is not my husband, he is my brother-in-law!'

'Your brother-in-law?' I stared at her. My mouth was hanging open and there was a low whining sound in my head like a million bees were nesting between my ears.

'Yes, my husband, Vikram's brother, was killed in an accident when my daughter was a little girl and so we came to live here, with Vikram.'

'Oh, that's nice… I mean, I'm really sorry about your husband.'

'Yes, Cassia, I am sorry too. Being a widow lady is not very nice, but Vikram is a kind, kind man. Now hold still and let your Auntie Lalitha finish this *mehandi*. From the look on your face I think we are both needing some milk and cookies!'

Call-Me-V

The next day, a tuk-tuk was parked ready for our trip to the spice market. So after cinnamon toast and mango juice at the guest house, Lula and I made our way through the human and animal traffic towards the trading district, Mattancherry.

We seemed to have escaped from Call-me-V, but instead of giving me all her attention in a good way, Lula was acting annoyed. She asked me why on earth I'd thought Vikram and Lalitha were married, which I said was a pretty dumb question, as they were the same age, lived in the same house and were both called Chaudhury.

We passed through a really old bit of Kochi in silence. Falling-down houses with trees growing out of the roofs lined the road. Looking through the padlocked, iron gates at the grand entrances I thought some seriously rich people must have lived here once and I wondered what had happened to them.

Why did they leave their houses to just fall down? If they didn't want them, then why didn't they let other people live in them?

I leaned out of the tuk-tuk as we passed a palace. The driver said the Portuguese built it five hundred years ago as a present for the king. It didn't look much older than the other buildings, but tourists and a party of local school kids were queuing on the stairs waiting for the doors to open.

I wanted to know more about Call-me-V, but I couldn't find the right words to ask my grown-up mum if this was a serious boyfriend thing or just a... what?

Serious relationships were all that adults did, wasn't it? And how did her being someone's girlfriend and my mum work when we were all together? What if I wanted ice-cream again? Would she let me or would it be Call-me-V's rules while we were here? What if he was really mean to me? Would Lula take my side or buddy up with him? And what if stuff happened that was more serious than ice-cream? Would she still love me?

We parked on Bazaar Road and started our buying expedition with perfumes. This was where Lula got the incense sticks and fragrance oils we sold in the shop. A red-and-black painted board outside the door listed all the different flowers they used in their mixtures. Tiny glass bottles lined the mirrored shelves of the shop.

The owner, Mrs Jaffrey, knew we were coming and she'd prepared a selection of new mixtures for Lula to try. The not-talking thing between me and Lula was making me feel sad and it was a relief not to be alone any more. We went in and slipped off our shoes.

Perched on a stool by the counter, drinking juice, I watched as Mrs Jaffrey laid out the sample bottles. Then she put small drops on to our skin and explained that each one was good for different things. Some were just perfumes, but others, like the massage oils, could help you feel better too. With some oils, like Rose, just the smell was enough to change your mood. I wondered if there was a mixture for difficult mothers.

Lula said she was looking for a bestseller and we sniffed and sighed our way through Green Orchid, Kerala Flower and something with juniper that Mrs Jaffrey said was very good for cellulite – I could see from Lula's expression that a couple of pints would be in the post before we left.

I tried to take charge of the order book, but Lula

took it off me and wrote down the orders as she went along. This was supposed to be my job and I was left sitting on the stool with no one talking to me and with nothing to do.

I was bored and fed up, but Lula loved trying to haggle over the prices. She started off with an insanely low offer, but Mrs Jaffrey wasn't playing. There was a bit of, 'I am just a poor shopkeeper' on both sides, but Mrs Jaffrey didn't cave. Lula tried hard, but I think the perfumes ended up way more expensive than she'd budgeted for.

Once we'd finished writing up the orders and arranging shipping, Mrs Jaffrey said she had a surprise and reached under the counter. She presented me with a tiny blue bottle with a silver lid and a purple tassel.

'Cassia, this is a very special perfume, I hope you will like it. It is a blend of Lotus for your smile, cinnamon for your name and even a bit of pepper for your energy.' She opened the bottle and passed it over to me.

I took a deep sniff and a sweet flowery smell curled up my nose. It made me think of Sunday mornings, when Lula lights incense sticks and we re-stock the shelves together. I suddenly felt homesick and I wanted to get out of the shop and be in the sun.

Our next stop was the ginger factory. It was built around a huge courtyard and the knobbly roots were laid out on the warm stone floor like a giant carpet. Lula said they would stay there, drying in the sun. They didn't have long to bake. The monsoon was due in another few months, and then this whole place would get a daily bath.

Lula bought a few samples for a catering business she'd started with some friends. At Christmas, Auntie Doré had said Lula should 'focus on the shop for pity's sake, Loopy Lu!'

'Well, I think it is time for lunch and a nice cup of tea,' Lula said, sounding more cheerful. I hoped she had got over her bad mood and was going to be nice to me for a while.

We found the tuk-tuk and made our way to the Spice Café. As we went inside I saw Call-me-V sitting at a table by the waterside. Of course, that was why she had cheered up. It was him she was happy to see, not me. Call-Me-V checked Lula's list in the order book. I tried to look over his shoulder.

'Have you talked to any of your friends at school yet, Cass?' Lula said it in a super-casual voice, but I didn't bite. I definitely didn't want to talk about that stuff in front of Call-Me-V.

'How's Auntie Doré getting on in the shop?' I said.

'Well, you know Doré, always ready with business advice,' Lula said in a really sarky voice.

'Maybe you should listen to her sometimes.'

'When I want advice like that I'll ask Cruella De Ville!'

'Yeah, cos she's available for a quick chat!'

'Cass, if Doré had her way, we wouldn't bother about organic, fair-trade or anything else. She thinks I'm daft to work the way I do and maybe she's right, but it's MY shop and I'll run it MY way or...'

She was blasting out a scary, goddess-level death-stare and had my hand in such a tight grip my fingers were turning blue.

'OK, I get the point, you can let go now,' I said.

She glanced down and gave the *mehandi* a good long look. 'Vikram has arranged tickets for a theatre show for us all. I told him you were interested in dancing. Isn't that nice of him, Cassia?' she said, looking all dolly-daydream at Call-me-V.

Actually a dance show sounded pretty cool, but I didn't want to go with him. I didn't even want to go with Lula. Didn't she realise what a terrible example she was setting? I knew he wasn't married or anything now, but everyone knew holiday romances were a disaster.

It was just like my *Peacock Spring* book. There was Una, falling in love with the poet, Ravi, and getting trashed by her stepmother, Alix. I was beginning to see why, for Una, going back to boarding school might look like a solid plan B.

On the way to the theatre Call-me-V explained that the style of the performance they were doing was called *Kathakali*. It was a mixture between a musical and a play and there weren't any words, as the actors sort of spoke with their hands and eyes. Call-me-V said they trained all their lives to learn the stories and the parts properly.

It was sounding a bit too old-school for me and I was beginning to wish I'd gone for belly-ache and a trip back to the guest house. But with our tickets, we got a card that explained the extreme facial expressions, which really helped to sort out what the characters were up to.

The performers got ready on stage and while they were doing their make-up Lula got her camera out.

Almost everyone in the cast was a God or Goddess, and the stories were all about the battle between heavenly worlds and demon worlds. All the actors were men, but they seemed to be making a real effort, aside from the coconut-shell boobs, which would have made some of Dad's theatre friends kind of hissy.

Lula put her camera away as people arrived to take their seats. The music started and everyone settled down. The story was introduced by the main singer. It was a demon woman versus heroic prince set-up and everyone who'd read the story knew that in about two hours' time it would end badly, for her.

Our seats were under the balcony and every few minutes a pistachio shell landed on the floor in front of me. I looked up and scanned the faces staring out at the stage. They were mostly in deep shadow, but a light from the stairs caught the pistachio-eater in silhouette. It looked like one of the little kids from Mr Rao's restaurant. He was drumming his hands in time to the music and this was sending shells spinning off the balcony railing.

'Look! It's your friends up there,' I said.

Lula looked up and shook her head. 'I don't think so.' Her chair scraped noisily along the floor as she twisted back to the stage, and the boy looked down.

He waved at me and put drinking straws into his mouth like a walrus. He looked so funny I couldn't help laughing. The people seated around us started shushing and Lula hissed, 'For Goodness' sake, Cassia, stop fidgeting.'

A shower of empty shells landed on my head and when I looked up again the boy was sitting on his mother's lap and the adults were all looking a bit annoyed.

At the interval, walrus boy came running up and offered me a handful of sweaty, green pistachios. I took a couple and cracked them open. I guessed his parents hadn't seen us because there was no sign of them downstairs or up on the balcony, and Lula was pacing about like she wanted to leave.

'Aren't you going to say hello to your friends?' I asked at the end of the show, as she walked straight towards the exit.

'No, Cass, I don't think that would be a good idea,' she said. Her face looked tight and witchy.

Just as we reached the doors, Mr and Mrs Met-at-the-Restaurant appeared. For a second they looked as uncomfortable as Lula, but then all the adults did this freakish face-morph thing and it was full-on 'How lovely to see you!' and 'Wasn't the show wonderful!'

Watching them, I almost believed everything was OK, until we were in the tuk-tuk going home and I felt Lula's hand. Her fingers were trembling and as cold as ice lollies.

Stupid O'clock and the
One Musketeer

It felt like the middle of the night when Lula cajoled me out of bed. I blundered about in a daze, trying to get dressed with my eyes closed. They cracked open once I reached the bathroom, but after a look at my scarecrow hair I shut them again.

Lula had decided on the public-transport option and we were booked on the early-morning commuter train that would take us up the coast, north to Kannur. It seemed Call-me-V was driving us as far as the station. But after that I was looking forward to it being just me and Lula again, for a while. As he loaded our bags, he showed me the triple-decker tiffin tins (India's completely brilliant version of the picnic hamper) stowed in the boot.

'My sister-in-law is worried you are not getting enough to eat, Cassia. She thinks you are having hollow legs and is blaming your mother for naming you after a tree!' he said.

We crossed the bridges back to the mainland and parked outside the railway station. The platform was like a zombie film, with sleepy people staggering on and off the train. Studenty tourists swung their enormous backpacks around like weapons of mass decapitation. Inside the carriage the aisles were packed with boys selling drinks, newspapers and snacks.

Call-me-V pushed on ahead and we Excuse-me'd our way to our seats. He seemed to be hanging around a bit, getting our cases up on the rack and ordering drinks. When the whistle blew I expected to see him make a run for the doors. But he settled himself down next to Lula and opened out a newspaper.

Once the train set off, Lula inflated a travel pillow and rested her head against the window. She looked really exhausted. A deep frown made a ridge between her eyes and she was twisting an earring as if it could grant her three wishes.

Perfect, just perfect. I thought I'd have Lula to myself for a bit. I really wanted to talk to her about school and stuff, but I couldn't while Call-me-V was poking his nose into our lives.

In London, Lula had kept saying things like 'When you get back to school, Cass', but I never wanted to go back. I couldn't go back.

I'd wanted to tell her about what was happening to me with Rachel and the other girls in the dance group loads of times. But lately, Lula had been so stressy and unpredictable, I was scared she'd throw a major emo fit and go stomping off to the headteacher, and then she'd find out I'd been skipping lessons and it would get even worse. All those times she thought I was at dance practice when really I was hiding out in the library.

I'd really hoped that here, in India, Lula would relax and things would go back to how they used to be, when I could tell her anything and she'd make it all right. She used to be Mrs Fixit, but recently she'd changed. I knew she couldn't just magic my problems away, but I did expect her at least to have time to listen. Now Call-me-V was always around and ruining everything.

I stared out of the window. The view of palm trees and fields reminded me of the plane journey coming over. It felt like a million years ago, and pretty much everything was different from what I'd expected. So much for escaping from my problems – it felt like I'd just got a whole new set to worry about.

I opened my book. Una was in trouble, too.

The governess, Alix, had gone a bit psycho because she had stolen whisky and Una thought she should tell the truth and not let a servant get sacked for it.

I felt a bit sorry for Alix (even though she was a horrible person) because her mum was Indian but her dad wasn't, and she didn't fit in with the English people or the Indians, and it made her scared and a bit mad. If Edward wasn't such an old-school dad it would probably have been OK. But he was too busy working to see what was happening.

Gradually everyone around me either fell asleep or pulled out laptops and started tippy-tapping away. We'd not been travelling long but my stomach was already rumbling. Lula and Call-me-V were dozing, so I took my tiffin box to the corridor between the carriages.

The train doors were left open and the countryside trundled slowly past in widescreen. I sat with my feet resting on the outside step and watched people start their day. A group of women were washing clothes in a river. Right next to them, others were cleaning cooking pots and bathing. I tried to imagine what it would be like not having your own bathroom. My mouth felt weird when I thought about cleaning my teeth in washing water.

Some kids playing football ran along beside the tracks, waving as the train passed. I leant out of the carriage and waved back at them.

We were going to stay with Lula's old college friend, Saachi. Lula said she had a daughter, Priyanka, who was my age, so there would be someone to hang out with at last. I'd thought about what she'd be like and I was sure she'd be really nice, and excited to have an English friend to teach her dance routines!

I'd wrapped up some colourful bracelets I'd found in a shop on Oxford street in tissue paper, and written *To my new friend, love Cass* on it in gold pen. I tried to picture Priyanka's face as she opened the package. She'd be really happy to have something pretty from a big city shop. She probably didn't have any proper fashionable stuff.

I tried to imagine what she would look like and how she would talk. I would lend her my iPod and she'd definitely want to hear all about my life in London. I wondered if she'd have her own room – probably not.

Perhaps she could come and stay with us some time. I could show her our flat, the telly, and the dishwasher. I could tell her about all the cool stuff me and my friends used to do at the weekends.

I wouldn't miss Rachel and the others at all if I had an Indian friend to show around.

The train lurched slightly as we crossed a gap in the tracks, and I felt the hard thump of the door swinging into my back. The jolt made me lose my footing on the outside step and, before I could do anything to stop myself, I was sliding slowly but surely into the view.

I scrabbled to get a grip on the floor, but my hands just skidded through the dust. Just as I was about to be pitched out of the train, there was a sharp pain in my arm and I felt a hand clamp my wrist in a tight hold. I opened my mouth to scream, but I was being dragged back through the dirt on my bum and all I heard was the train door as it slammed shut behind me.

'That was very foolish.' A local boy, about my age, was staring down at me. 'You might have been killed and you have made me spill my *chai*.'

He had dropped one of the paper cups he was carrying and it lay crumpled on the ground. Puddles of milky Indian tea had formed around his feet and mixed with the dirt on the train floor. The unappetising brew was sloshing in my direction.

I tried to stand up but my legs suddenly wouldn't

work properly. As I looked up at him, he took a step closer and I leaned away, pressing my back against the sharp edge of the carriage door.

'Here,' he said, and handed me a cup half-full of warm *chai*.

My hands were shaking too much to hold the cup properly, and as I gulped down a mouthful, I felt some dribble down my chin and on to my T-shirt.

The boy was still staring down at me. 'Where are you coming from?' he said.

'Kochi.'

'No, your native place.'

'Oh, London.' My throat felt tight and my voice sounded a bit squeaky.

'If you are ever wanting to get back, you must fasten the door properly.'

'Sorry,' I squeaked again.

'What is your name, girl from London?'

'Cassia.'

'Hello, Cassia, my name is Porthos.'

'Really? Like in *The Three Musketeers*?'

'No! Really my name is Dev. I just like the story.' He was smiling now. 'May I sit with you?'

'I've got some food. We could share it,' I said, pointing to Auntie Lalitha's picnic.

I was covered in dirt and his clothes weren't exactly designer, but there was a newspaper in the bin which I unfolded on to the floor. The spilled chai soaked through in patches, but at least it wasn't running all over the carriage. I mopped my hands on my jeans and unsnapped the lid of the tiffin tin. On the top layer sat three coconut cookies. I passed one over to the boy and, as the sugar hit my stomach, I started feeling less shaky.

'What do you do, Cassia?'

'I help my mum with our shop.'

He was staring at me. I felt my face getting hotter. I didn't know if it was shock or because he was really handsome. Maybe this was how Lula felt when she looked at Call-me-V. That thought made me feel shaky again. I took another big gulp of chai.

'Why are you not at school?'

'I'm going to be a dancer.'

'How will you learn to dance if you don't study?'

'I don't mean ballet, I like more modern stuff like street dance and Bollywood.'

'Really?' Dev said with a puzzled look.

'Yes, really! What do you want to do?'

'Computers and world-class cricket,' he said. 'But for now my job is to rescue foolish tourist girls.'

'Thank you for saving me.'

'That is OK, you are nearly family.'

'What do you mean?'

'Your *mehandi*. I can see from the initials that you will be marrying my grandfather.'

'Ha ha! Mr Lifesaver!'

He stared out of the window, rubbing at the dust on the glass with his fingers. I thought he was going to say something else, but he must have changed his mind.

We had pulled into a station and I realised it was time to go back to my seat. I thought about spending the rest of my holiday with Lula and Call-me-V and for a few seconds I imagined running away with Dev instead. He was probably sitting in third class, but I expected it was more fun there with people chatting and hanging out. Maybe I'd make some new friends.

Then I remembered Saachi's daughter would be waiting in Malabar, and I imagined giving her the bracelets and swimming in the sea all day and teaching her how to dance like me. She'd be so disappointed if I didn't show up.

'Goodbye, Mr Musketeer. I have to go now.'

'*Chal*, goodbye, Cassia from London. I will tell my grandfather he is making a good match.'

I watched as he disappeared down the corridor. Then I carefully flattened the paper cup and put it into the pocket of my jeans.

Lula and Call-me-V were awake when I got back to our seats. He dragged our cases off the racks and we Excuse me'd our way towards the exit. Dev had gone and the sticky puddle of *chai* was already evaporating in the midday heat.

I got off the train feeling very crumpled and a bit sweaty. The platform was heaving with people, but no one seemed to be in a hurry.

'Good grief, Cass, look at you! How on earth did you get that mucky on a train?' Lula asked.

I looked down at my torn, dust-coated jeans and filthy finger-nails. How many layers of shoe dirt had they scraped up as I slid towards a mangling on the tracks? And what if Dev hadn't been there?

Princess Priyanka

We took a taxi from the station to the village. Call-me-V sat in the front, chatting with the driver. He hadn't brought any bags with him, but it looked like he would be hanging around for a while longer. I wondered if this was just part of his looking-after-us job or because he and Lula had a romance going on. I expect she paid him really well – maybe that was why he was sticking so close to her.

The taxi stopped in front of a wooden building. Windows set high into the walls reflected birds squawking in the surrounding trees. It looked like a really massive garden shed.

'Is this where they live?' I asked.

'Oh no, Cass, Saachi's house is right down by the beach. This is one of Vikram's new projects. He wanted us to see it before it gets renovated.'

Call-me-V took a key out of his pocket and fitted it into a padlock on the door. The wood creaked and the door swung open on a dusty room.

'This used to be a candle-making workshop – the old equipment has to be cleared out. But isn't it a lovely space, Cass?' Lula was practically skipping about and I could tell she had her decorator head on.'Vikram's got great plans for this building,' she said.

I looked around at the shed. It didn't even have a proper floor. Hanging from hooks on the wall were big metal cooking pots and a thick layer of wax was caked on the wooden workbench. I ran my thumbnail across the yellow lumps and the smell of honey seeped into the air. Although it was a dump, the smell in the shed reminded me of Auntie Doré's super-cool dining room with its rows of expensive scented candles.

I wondered if Call-me-V was rich like Auntie Doré. He didn't look rich, but maybe rich people in India acted the same as everyone else. What did he do, besides driving Lula about? I tried not to stare as I imagined him in an office like Dad's, or at a really fancy restaurant with friends.

He glanced over at Lula and I swear she actually blushed. This was getting gruesome, worse than gruesome. Lula skipped about a bit more, talking about earth-tone palettes and rustic surfaces while Call-me-V smiled at her like she was the most wonderful thing he'd ever seen. Then, from her handbag Lula produced a packet of incense sticks.

'Ah, you think we should have a *Puja*, Luella, m'n?' said Call-me-V. He passed her a tiny elephant statue attached to his keys. 'I will get some flowers,' he said and walked out.

'What is a *Puja*?' I said.

'A sort of spiritual housewarming, and request to the Gods for help with our new enterprise.' She looked wistful when she said it, and then her face went all pink again as Call-me-V came back in with a bunch of blooms I'd seen hanging from a tree by the door. They put the statue on the workbench and laid the flowers in front of it.

'We must wash our hands first,' said Call-me-V, opening a rusty tap on the wall.

Brownish water dribbled into a bucket on the floor. It took a while to run clear and they both rinsed their hands. I stuck my hands in my pockets. Then Lula lit the incense and waved the scented smoke in the air while Call-me-V muttered some stuff I couldn't understand. When I couldn't stand any more, I sat outside, watching the taxi driver smoke cigarettes and talk on his mobile phone. He was having a huge argument with someone.

Lula and Call-me-V came out eventually, and we got back in the taxi. I sat in the front this time and the driver found a music station to listen to. I asked him to turn it up really loud, but even though I couldn't hear Lula and Call-me-V, I could see them reflected in the rear-view mirror, scribbling drawings and numbers and stuff in the shop order book.

I wondered what they were doing. The shop wasn't Call-me-V's business, it was Lula's. But when they did the shed *Puja*, Lula talked about *their* new enterprise like it had something to do with her, too.

Lula's friend, Saachi, and her daughter, Priyanka, were standing outside their house waiting to meet us. Parked in the drive was a car that made the Green Goddess look like a joke.

When I saw Priyanka, looking like something straight off a film poster, my heart dropped into my grubby shoes and stayed there. I knew the train journey hadn't done my outfit any favours, but compared with Priyanka I looked like a charity advert. Why hadn't Lula told me she was rich, beautiful, perfect?

Lula was so pleased to see her that she nearly

knocked her over. 'Look at you, bonny girl! You've grown so much since last time I saw you. This is my daughter, Cassia,' she said, pushing me forward.

Priyanka smiled and smoothed down the spotless silk top stretched tight over her round stomach. Her long, super-straight, advert-perfect hair was pulled back into a clip that matched the colours of her outfit. She had a friendly smile, but I saw her staring at my torn jeans. I tried to force myself to smile back, but my mouth wouldn't work properly.

Saachi said, 'Hello, Cassia, I've heard so much about you,' and, 'Don't you look like your dad!' And then she suggested we all go inside to freshen up.

I thought Lula would introduce Call-me-V, but it was obvious pretty quickly that they all knew each other already. I was the only new person, the stranger, the one who needed to be introduced.

It felt like Lula had this secret Kerala life that I had just barged into. And now, as we walked into the massive marble hallway, she was practising her Malayalam with Priyanka while Saachi talked with Call-me-V. Everyone was talking and smiling at each other – everyone except me.

If Rachel hadn't been so angry with me I'd be at school now, and all this would be going on a million miles away. I betted that Lula would have preferred it. Then she could have hung out with perfect Priyanka instead of me, with my grubby clothes and rubbish hair.

Priyanka's room was at the back of the house. From her balcony there was a postcard-perfect view of the sea. I put my scruffy suitcase on the guest bed. The present I'd got her was in the bottom of my wash-bag. As I looked around the room, I could see she already had loads of much prettier bracelets just heaped up on her dressing table. She had lots of other stuff I hadn't expected her to have too. I left the wash-bag in my case. Why would she be interested in my rubbish present?

Priyanka wanted to show me round, but I just wanted to get to get away from everyone, including her. I unpacked my swimming costume and stomped down to the water with Priyanka following behind.

'Don't go out too far, Cassia. Actually, it is quite dangerous once you get past the breakers!' Priyanka called out in a bossy voice as I marched across the sand.

I ignored her and ran as fast as I could into the water. I would show her. I body-surfed a couple of small waves, landing gently back in the shallows. Priyanka sat neatly on the sand like one of Lula's plump and very pretty sofa cushions.

The sky was a bright, clear blue and I floated on my back to watch the tiniest of clouds float by. Now this was more like it, I thought, as I ducked and splashed about in the warm, salty water. Maybe I could just stay in the sea for ever and forget about everything until it was time to go home. But then I remembered things were completely rubbish there, too.

'Stop fooling around, Cassia. There is a big wave coming!' Priyanka shouted.

I turned to look. She was wrong about the wave. It wasn't big, it was VERY big.

I tried to dive under the swell, but it caught me full in the belly and knocked me off my feet. I tumbled over and over in the pounding water. All the air had been punched out of my lungs, my chest was aching and I was starting to think seriously about panicking. Then, its fun done, the ocean dumped me on the beach like a sack of wet washing. I spat out a mouthful of fish-bath. Through my stinging eyes I could see Priyanka laughing at me. I emptied sand out of my costume.

Priyanka handed me a beach towel as I dragged myself out of the water. I must have looked even more pathetic than when I arrived. Had she waited to tell me about the wave until it was too late? At least the scouring had got my hands clean.

The *mehandi* had faded a little, too, and that made me think of Jonny Gold and Dev and being rescued, and I started to feel very sorry for myself and had to go back to the sea to splash more water on my face.

Priyanka kept talking to me about how great it was to meet me at last, but for a while I pretended the water in my ears had made me deaf. I knew I was being mean, but I couldn't stop. She just wasn't what I was expecting.

I lay face-down on the sand and let the hot sun bake me dry. I hoped it would burn out the bad feeling that was building up in my stomach. I really needed a friend, someone who would like me, so why did I get landed with Princess Perfect who had all the jewellery she needed and didn't like swimming?

When we got back to the house, Priyanka told me Saachi had arranged a *Welcome to the Malabar* party and that some of the neighbours were invited. She said she would fix my hair and lend me an Indian outfit until

I got my crumpled clothes sorted out. She had chosen a long top and baggy trousers she called a *salwar kameez* in emerald green, to 'complement my eyes'.

Of course it also matched the shade of envy I felt when I saw her amazing collection of clothes. It was in three sections, one she called 'sarees-for-the-aunties', then there was a rack of *salwar* tops for everyday over jeans and, just to make me feel really tragic, she had a western, designer selection for holidays abroad. None of it had any creases, rips, loose threads, or stains of any kind. It was also grouped and ranked by colour and shade.

She laid the outfit on my bed and waited for me to try it on. Even though it was really pretty I didn't want to wear it, but she kept on at me until I agreed, just to shut her up.

'What is this grunge-meets-high-street look you favour, Cassia? Is it very on-trend in the UK right now?' she asked, watching me dress.

'Yeah,' I replied. 'All the celebs are leaving their clothes scrunched up in a bag for a week before they wear them.'

'It must be fabulous to be so close to the heart of fashion, Cassia.'

'Yes. It's terrific,' I said.

The party wasn't totally in our honour. There was something going on in the village that had everyone up a height, and Saachi had got a protest group started. She and Lula had been deep in 'Do you remember when…' ever since we'd arrived, so Call-me-V and Princess Priyanka had taken over as party-planners, with me as their scruffy assistant.

Working from a hand-written, double-sided list (yes, that's right, a list!), we arranged chairs out on the veranda and set a row of anti-mosquito coils burning. Multi-coloured paper lanterns hung in the garden and we filled them with tea-lights. Priyanka had arranged with her mum that we could have a canopy in the garden for the 'young folk', and we carried out rugs and cushions from the house.

All the guests were bringing food and something to drink, so by early evening all we had left to do was cut and clean the banana palm leaves we would use as plates. This was a super-green solution for party plates and best of all, no washing-up! Of course, first someone had to shimmy up a palm tree and hack off a couple of branches and it seemed I'd been volunteered.

Priyanka pointed to the rope foot-rests circling the trunk at regular stages. The palm tree was bent over, and towards the top the trunk ran almost parallel to the ground.

I scrambled up to the first support and then, gripping the trunk with my legs, I hauled myself along to the second and then the third rung. Apart from getting properly bruised knees, it was pretty easy. A few more hefts and I'd reached the top of the trunk. The penknife Priyanka gave me was wedged in my back pocket, and as I twisted round to get it I looked down.

Priyanka and Lula were watching me from the garden. 'Can you see any bananas yet, Cass?' Lula called up.

I tilted my head back and looked into the leaves. There were no bananas. Instead there was a generous bunch of what even I recognised were coconuts.

'Banana palms are the other side of the house, Cass,' Lula laughed.

In fact, they both laughed quite a lot. Priyanka's 'hilarious prank' was obviously a family favourite.

I decided to stay in the tree for a bit. My eyes were still stinging from the sea-water, but from up high I could see the ocean and the beach, girls playing netball, and the white birds picking flies off the buffaloes' backs.

'Come on down, Cass,' Lula called. 'There's a lime soda ready in the kitchen.'

I didn't reply.

Once they had gone back inside, I climbed down and took a long shower. I just left my hair to sprout as usual. I looked at the green top Priyanka had laid out for me and I even held it up in front of the mirror. She was right, the colour did look really nice with my eyes, but I couldn't wear it – I was too upset about the coconut joke. So I put it back in her wardrobe.

I had thought Priyanka would be more ordinary and that she'd like me and I'd feel like the special one. But instead I felt like a stupid, frizzy-haired lump, whose mum laughed at her because she couldn't even tell a banana tree from a coconut.

As it got dark, the guests started arriving, all loaded up with dishes of steaming rice, fish, coconut-scented curry and boxes of sweets.

Lula had made some chocolate cup-cakes as our contribution. Priyanka saw them and I heard her say, 'Oh Goodness, Auntie Luella, those do look delicious!'

Lula beamed at her with pleasure.

I watched Priyanka's face as she carefully picked one out. Maybe she'd been warned about Lula's cooking because I noticed she only broke off a tiny piece before setting the cup-cake down again.

The food table was getting crowded with people arranging their contributions. Everyone was very glamorously dressed – except for me. I hadn't packed anything partyish so I was stuck in jeans and T-shirt. Priyanka's loaned *salwar* would have been perfect.

As a full moon rose above the trees, a group of musicians appeared and set up their instruments in the middle of the garden. They had brought two kinds of drum and a sitar. The neighbour's children taught me a routine from their favourite film, so I showed them a few street-dance moves which made them laugh a lot, and after a bit of practising we twirled and stomped our way round the garden.

Dancing cast a spell on me. Christmas, school and mean girls floated away into the moonlight. This would be what my life would be like every day when I was older, and on TV. There'd be dancing and parties and glamour, and Jonny Gold and his band playing just for me.

As soon as everyone had cleared their plates, Saachi asked the musicians to take a break. And once the garden had gone quiet, she started to speak. I could tell by people's expressions that it was all serious stuff and she had to keep stopping as angry muttering broke out. Priyanka did a whispered translation of the most important bits and I thought I got the picture.

A developer had bought a big piece of land along the beachfront and was building a luxury hotel complex on the cliffs. The mangrove trees, which protected the coast from flooding, would be cut down, the beach would be fenced off and many of the villagers would lose their homes. The developers wouldn't talk to anyone from the village and no one was sure where their money was coming from.

Saachi had been doing some investigating through her legal contacts and she was trying to find out who was behind the scheme. Anyway, everyone had got their angry heads on and Saachi got a round of applause for her efforts. Lula did a little speech about how much she loved Kerala, Call-me-V beamed a big smile at her, and the adults got all teary-eyed about shared values and blah-de-blah.

I sat by myself and listed to the waves rolling on to the beach. It sounded like Saachi had done loads of research and I wondered why she cared so much. It wasn't like her mansion house would be going anywhere.

Oh, Still My Beating Heart!

The next morning at breakfast there was no sign of Call-me-V and I guessed he'd left after the party. I wondered if he'd gone back to Kochi or maybe he had a guest house near here, too.

Lula was only picking at her toast and she kept twisting her earrings round and round. Maybe she was missing him already. Poor Lula, I'd never thought she might be lonely before. She'd been by herself since Dad went.

A year before he left, he covered a story about two male penguins in New York zoo who'd become a couple. They even pretended a small rock was an egg and took turns to sit on it. When they turned the story into a book, he got it for me for Christmas. I was little then, and he used to sit on the end of my bed and read it. He did all the voices and everything. I suppose that's when he realised he wanted to live a different life. I knew he still cared about me and my mum, but we weren't enough any more.

I hated hearing them fighting and the things they said didn't make sense until much later. When Lula explained that Dad was leaving us because he had fallen in love with another man, I asked her if he would still love me when I grew up, even though I was a girl. She hugged me until I practically couldn't breathe.

But Lula would be OK. She was with me and Saachi and Priyanka now, so she wouldn't miss Call-me-V for long. We were going fabric-buying later, just the two of us, and I decided I would be super-nice and helpful to show her that she didn't need him around any more.

Priyanka's grandma, Granny-ji, arrived while we were eating. She poured some tea, 'the cup that cheers', and asked me if I was feeling 'in the pink'. I replied that I wasn't quite sure.

Saachi explained that she used to be an English teacher and gave lessons to families in the village, using old children's books. Saachi said that for years she'd believed that Enid Blyton's Famous Five were real British kids. I wondered if she missed being a teacher now she was old and I promised to send over some top-quality, modern teen-lit. Then Granny-ji patted her chest and said, 'Oh, still my beating heart!' which made Lula laugh so much she spilt her coffee.

Saachi told Lula that Priyanka still hadn't decided on what career path she was going to follow, but that she was seriously considering Law.

'*Amma*, you're so boring! You think everyone should study Law.' Priyanka pushed her breakfast away, uneaten, which was really rude of her.

'There's nothing wrong with being boring, Priya. As a matter of fact, if you work hard, you can make a difference in the world, you know.'

'*Amma*! I want a profession with much more stylish outfits.'

I saw Lula smile, but I thought Priyanka was being a spoilt brat.

Saachi didn't reply, but she looked a bit cross.

Priyanka asked me what I wanted to do and I told her about being a dancer. She said girls here went to dancing school when they were really young, and studied for years if they wanted to do it seriously. Things were different in London, I said. Then I explained about helping Lula in the shop, too. I saw Lula and Saachi exchange a look and no one said anything after that.

We cleared the table and got ready to go out. Saachi offered to give us a lift into town. I thought Priyanka was going to school, but she appeared from her room holding a sketch-pad. Apparently, Princess Priya had taken the day off and Lula seemed really pleased. So it wasn't going to be just the two of us after all.

I shut the door of our room with a bang. It wasn't fair. Lula was my mum, not hers. I didn't see why Lula wanted her to tag along. I could help, but Priyanka didn't know anything about the shop.

As we cleared the hill out of the village, I saw the site of the hotel development. Saachi asked if we wanted to take a closer look and stopped the car at the side of the road. Priyanka stayed in the car with Lula, but I followed Saachi up the path.

The building site looked empty, and we walked beside the wire fence which went all the way around the plot. Golden bricks, like chunks of cinder toffee, were stacked in neat piles against the edges. The complete circuit took us to the edge of the cliff overlooking the sea.

Whoever ended up staying in this hotel was going to get an amazing view, I thought. I wondered how

I'd feel if I was a rich person wanting a beach holiday. Would I care about a few mangroves and some village houses? I could definitely picture Auntie Doré here, that was for sure. I walked over to the board with the artist's impression on it.

'Wow! Saachi, come and look!' I called.

She followed me over and stared up at the drawing.

The picture of the tall glass tower had been partly covered in spray paint and the words BEARS BEWARE were graffitti'd over it in gold. Someone had done a very careful job on the letters, even though the words didn't make much sense.

'But I do not understand… there are no bears near here,' Saachi said.

The name of the investment company, Auramy Incorporated, was just visible through the paint.

'Wouldn't it be nice to have a hotel with shops and restaurants here, Saachi?'

'As a matter of fact, I don't mind them building a hotel. Tourists bring money and jobs. But this is not the right place. The costs to the people and the environment are much too high.' She looked so fierce when she said it, like the Goddess Kali gone nuclear, I felt a bit sorry for Auramy Incorporated when she caught up with them.

'When did you decide to be a lawyer, Saachi?'

'When I was old enough to notice how the rich treat the poor.'

'Do you think Priyanka will feel the same as you?'

'Priya notices only frocks at the moment, I'm afraid. And what about you, Cassia, why do you want to be a dancer?'

I started to answer her, telling her stuff about fame, and parties and being on TV, but somehow saying it out loud to Saachi, it didn't feel real any more. I couldn't find the right words and my voice didn't sound like I really meant it.

I stopped talking and felt my face go red. She probably thought I was an idiot. But she wasn't looking at me with a for-goodness'-sake expression, she was really interested and was taking my answer seriously.

I managed to mumble something about how being part of the dance group, us all working together to put on a show, connected me to something bigger than myself.

Then she smiled and nodded her head. 'That is how the law feels for me, too. Putting something right in the world, even something quite small, makes me feel that what I do matters and that I matter, too. You know, we have more in common than you might imagine, Cassia.' She linked arms with me and we walked away from the building site together.

When we got back to the car, I saw Priyanka passing Lula her sketch-book. They had their heads together while Priyanka turned the pages, showing Lula drawings of wedding dresses and pictures cut from fashion magazines.

As I climbed into the back seat, Lula closed the sketch-book. I wanted to tell her about seeing the graffiti, but seeing her snap the book closed made me feel shut out. Like there was a secret between her and Priyanka and I wasn't included.

The weaving workshop was just how Lula had described it. Piles of fabric parcels labelled with exotic destinations filled the office like giant sugar cubes.

Back at the shop, my Saturday job was to check the delivery and carefully cut through the stitching that held the parcels together. Then we'd go through each bale of fabric and check it against the order book.

The packaging was covered with colourful customs stamps and it seemed a waste to just chuck it away. I'd had the idea of turning it into carrier bags for the shop. I'd cut out big squares, making sure to get a bit of the coloured customs stamps on each panel. Then I stitched them together with waxed thread. Making the bags was how I earned my allowance.

When we moved out of the office and into the busy weaving shed, it became very hot even though all the windows were open and fans whirled in the roof. Lula looked at the colours on the wooden weaving machine while the man operating it tugged on a string, making the thread fly from side to side.

I watched his feet, as he controlled the up and down criss-crossing of the cotton with foot pedals. The fabric appeared really slowly, line by line. I realised that this was where Lula's ideas turned into real stuff and, watching her face, I could see how much she loved it.

The weaver was sweating and taking big drinks of water as he worked. He said his kids wanted to move to Bangalore and get office jobs where they would get better money and proper holidays. Lula said she'd heard about all the call-centres, 'summoning the young like the Pied Piper'. Then she laughed and said she expected to be talking to his kids about her overdraft some day soon.

After the first few centimetres of fabric were visible, Lula looked relieved and I guessed the sample was working OK. We all went back into the design room and the manageress got out a book full of fabric squares. This fabric was much finer than the material Lula usually got for cushion covers and bedspreads.

Priyanka kept holding pieces against our skin, then making notes in her sketch-book. She picked out an emerald green square which changed colour to a soft pink when it caught the light, and held it against my face, then she and Lula made a sort of death-by-chocolate-delicious noise together and Priyanka scribbled in the sketch-book again.

They obviously didn't want me hanging about, and I really needed a cold drink, so I left them to it. There were shops on the road, but after my *Odomos* humiliation I was a bit nervous about setting off alone.

'Are you looking for something?' The manageress was standing beside me.

'I'd like to get something to drink.'

'I am arranging to get *chai* for your mother – would you like one, too?'

'OK.'

I must have sounded a bit disappointed because she said, 'The shop sells drinks out of the fridge. Maybe you would prefer cola or a lemonade?'

'Oh, that would be great!'

She told me how to say 'Please' and 'How much?' and I set off up the road, practising *'Dayavuchetu'* and *'Etra*?' under my breath the whole way.

The boy working in the shop looked a bit like Dev, and when I tried out the words the manageress had taught me he smiled, which made me blush, and then I got so embarrassed about blushing that I started to choke on my drink. My eyes watered and cola was leaking out of my nose.

He stopped smiling and looked really worried. It probably wasn't good for business to have a customer explode in your shop. Seriously, why was I such a freak? I would never make friends here, or anywhere else.

Maybe Rachel had done some kind of voodoo curse on me from London. After all, I had nearly fallen out of a train, practically drowned, and now I was choking to death. It wouldn't be so bad if it had all happened in private, but someone was always there, watching me. Though if Dev hadn't come along I'd be a train-mangled freak, which was worse.

I wondered where Dev was now – a million miles away, probably. Maybe he was busy rescuing another girl-in-peril. That thought made my throat close up again.

My eyes were watering really badly now and the boy handed me a packet of tissues from the counter. I ripped the wrapper open and buried my boiling face in a nest of cotton. I stood very still, gasping and wheezing until my breathing got normal, then I tried another sip of Coke. The bubbles helped and I set the bottle back on the counter, which was stacked high with that day's Indian newspapers.

Staring up at me from the front page, I saw super-handsome Jonny Gold's picture. My breathing went funny and I quickly swallowed the last of the drink. I had no idea what the story was about, but I had just enough rupees left to buy a copy so I put the money on the counter and rushed back to the weaving workshop.

Saachi's car was pulling up by the entrance when I got back, and Priyanka and Lula stood waiting by the door. They were chatting together and Priyanka had a parcel tucked under her arm. I could see bits of fabric sticking out of it. I wondered if they'd even noticed I'd been gone. I tore out the Jonny Gold article and stuffed it into the pocket of my jeans. I had no idea how I would read the story, but I certainly didn't want to share Jonny Gold with Priyanka.

Back at the house, I ran to my room and grabbed my swimming costume. Priyanka was in the kitchen when I got downstairs, but her sketch-book was lying on a table in the hallway.

I picked it up and started flicking through the pages. In the beginning it was all traditional English wedding dresses, big meringues of white satin and little kids in pink. Then, as I flicked through, the pictures got more Indian-looking, more colourful, with layers and beautiful patterns printed on to the fabric. I could see Priyanka was really good at drawing - no wonder Lula made a fuss of her.

I felt a stab of jealousy and turned to the middle of the book. Even the faces on the figures looked lifelike – and weirdly familiar. There was a picture of a pale girl in an emerald saree-style dress, and standing next to her was an Indian girl in blue with advert-perfect hair. Underneath, in very neat writing it said, *The Bridesmaids*.

The book suddenly felt very heavy in my hands. I turned the next page. In the same neat handwriting Priyanka had spelled out *Auntie Luella and Uncle Vikram-ji's Wedding!* And underneath the words, in a beautiful pink-and-orange dress, was a picture of Lula, my mum, Auntie Luella, smiling and happy, and standing beside her was the bridegroom, Call-me-V.

Dramarama

The air in the room suddenly popped and then everything fell away. I had walked over a cliff, cartoon-style. Only it wasn't a cartoon, it was real, and I wasn't running in mid-air, I was falling fast.

The next few minutes were a kind of raging blur. I remember tearing the pages out of Priyanka's stupid sketch-book and throwing them around like confetti. Then there was Priyanka shouting, 'Stop it, Cassia!' and Lula telling me to calm down, and then stomach-ache-sick-making crying until Saachi shut me in her office and put the phone in my hand. In the background I could hear Priyanka's angry voice and Lula saying, 'I'm so sorry' over and over.

It took a few rings before Dad picked up. Then I heard his deep voice mumbling down the phone and I almost started bawling again.

'Hi, Dad.'

'Hello, kiddo, what's up?'

'How do you know something's up?'

'Dad radar. Is there trouble in paradise?'

'Yeah.'

'Hot-chocolate-with-marshmallows trouble, or Dad-get-your-passport trouble?'

'It's an even worse kind, Dad.'

'Deep breaths, Cass, and tell me all about it.'

So I did. I didn't want to hurt him, but I told him about Lula and Call-me-V and their embarrassing secret romance and how I'd found the Indian wedding pictures in the sketch-book.

I told him how left out of everything I felt, like everything was being organised in secret. How scared I was about life here being so different from my life in London. How I missed watching TV and eating heat-and-eat-food. How lonely it made me feel when I didn't understand what people were saying and how stupid I felt when I didn't know how stuff worked – I couldn't even shop properly!

I told him about the scabby dog I'd seen and the lady without proper fingers, how no one was allowed to wear shorts or eat ice-cream, how the train doors were really, really dangerous and the way some people had big houses and laptops and some people washed their clothes in the river.

Dad laughed. 'Rich people live differently to poor people all over the world, Cass. Your mum loves you, Cass. She didn't do any of this to hurt you.'

'Did you know already, too?'

'Yes, kiddo.'

'But why didn't anyone tell me, Dad?'

'Because you were so unhappy at school, sweetie, and your mum thought it was best if you met everyone and got to know them first, with no pressure.'

'But Call-me-V isn't like you, Dad.'

'You mean Vikram? I hope not, for your poor mum's sake, sweetie!'

'I don't mean the gay thing. But I can't call him Dad instead of you.'

'You don't have to. Just call him Vikram. He is a good man, Cass, and he really loves your mum.'

'Dad! Did you get him checked out or something?'

'Oh, yes. I can't have my precious girls getting mixed up with a creepster! Was it a nice dress, the one Priyanka designed for you?'

'Yeah, I suppose... actually, Dad, it was really pretty. She must hate me now.'

'Probably not. Go and say your sorries, Cass. It will be OK, you know, in the end.'

He sounded so sure and I really wanted to believe him. But I'd made a total idiot of myself and Priyanka was really angry.

'Everything will feel better soon, Cass, I promise. Now, it's still stupid o'clock here and I need my beauty sleep.'

'OK, bye Dad, I love you.'

'Love you back, kiddo.'

I held the phone close to my ear until the line clicked out. Talking to Dad made me feel a bit better. I wanted to believe him about everything being OK, but I wasn't sure.

I had stopped crying, but I wasn't ready to face anyone in the house yet. I sneaked out on to the terrace and ran along the beach. My chest hurt from shouting and my face was covered in dried snot and salty tears.

I dunked my head in the warm water and tried to wash away all the lonely, angry sadness that filled my head. Maybe I should just go home. Catch a plane back to London and stay with Dad for a bit, maybe for ever. Lula could stay here with Call-me-V and Priyanka could be her replacement daughter. She'd probably do a better job of it than me.

I'd walked away from the sea now, and ended up

on the edge of the village by a children's play park. Small kids scooted around me on their way to the swings. I was just sitting, slumped on the slide, staring into space when I heard a familiar voice beside me.

'Are you in distress again, Cassia, girl from London?'

I was half expecting it to be a trauma-related hallucination, but when I opened my eyes Dev was smiling down in full 3D. My heart sort of flip-flopped and I found myself grinning like the little kids twirling on the roundabout.

'What are you doing here?'

'I live here!'

'Oh, Dev. I wish you could drag me out of trouble this time.'

'Perhaps another cup of *chai*?'

'You sound like my mum. She believes warm beverages have magical properties!'

'You should listen to your *amma*. They are usually right about such things.'

'You haven't met mine! Would you like to go for a walk?'

'First, I must check my sister is at practice.'

'What's she practising?'

'Come with me and you can see, London girl.'

We walked through the back streets of the village. The houses here were very different to Saachi's. We passed people sitting outside, preparing food. They were waving flies away from the dishes and keeping dust from scudding up into the pans. It was weird seeing people cooking on the roadside, but then I thought it wasn't really so different from a BBQ in the back garden – which Lula really loves even though we always end up with burgers garnished with bits of grass and flies floating in the squash. I wondered if this was just a short-cut or if Dev lived here.

We came to an open square by a school. Set up in the middle was a dusty netball court. Close up, I could see that faded lines marked out a rather uneven playing surface. The hoops were cut from old metal drums, and neatly plaited strips of multi-coloured plastic made the nets.

A game was going on and the two teams of girls were in full match voice. I couldn't understand what they were saying but it sounded pretty fierce.

A girl in a blue bib, with GS stitched on it, looked up as we arrived and waved cheerily at Dev. Seeing me, she nudged some of her team mates and the game slowly came to a stop. The girl came over to us and then she and Dev started waggling their fingers at each other. It was like watching the Kathakali dancers again, and I realised they must be doing sign language.

'Cassia, I would like you to meet my little sister, Nandita. She is the team captain.'

'Hi, I play netball at school, too,' I said.

She looked questioningly at Dev. He signed something to her and she smiled.

'She is saying you are very tall, but are you any good at shooting?'

'I used to play a mean Goal Attack...'

Nandita smiled and led me on to the court. She sent one of the girls off and handed me a blue bib. Then she pointed to our goal end and the game started again. It took me a while to get warmed up, and until I'd been barged a few times I was ridiculously polite. But, after a few pointy elbows had hit home, I got some good passes across the circle to Nandita and even had a couple of shots at goal myself.

Our team was already ahead, but when I dropped a ball cleanly through the hoop from the edge of the circle I got big high-fives off the rest of the team. Through it all, Nandita was totally focused on the game and the whole team watched her for direction. She reminded me of Rachel at rehearsals, getting everyone working, but making the hard work feel like fun.

After half an hour, I was completely exhausted and dripping with sweat, but I hadn't stopped smiling the whole time. I hadn't been with a big group of laughing girls for ages. The last time I saw the dance group, no one had been laughing.

The girl on the sidelines blew a whistle and the game stopped. Everyone piled off the court to get drinks out of their bags.

Dev handed me a bottle of water, and laughed at something his sister signed. 'Nandita is saying you can stay on the team, if you like.'

'That would be so great!'

'It is a pity the court will not be here for very long,' said Dev, frowning.

'What do you mean?'

'This space is to be a car park for the new hotel.'

'What will Nandita's team do then?'

'We do not know.'

I watched Nandita packing up the netball kit. The other girls were starting to walk home now. They strolled away, chatting, arms linked together. I watched them go, wishing they were my friends and we were all going off together for pizza and a Coke somewhere.

'Has your sister always been deaf?'

'No. When she was little, there was a tidal wave where we lived and it washed away our house. Nandi was in the water for a long long time and afterwards she could not hear any more.'

'Do you mean the Tsunami?' I remembered Lula crying at the pictures on TV, trees and cars floating away into the sea.

'Sport is not just a timepass thing, it is very important to her.' He was bouncing the ball hard on the ground as he spoke. It made a hard, slapping sound on his skin as he caught it.

'I have to go now, Dev, but I know someone who is trying to stop the development. Maybe she can help?'

'That is kind, Cassia, but rich people usually get what they want.'

I remembered what Saachi said about how the rich treat the poor and how it made her want to be a lawyer. 'You can trust Saachi!' I said.

Dev showed me how to say 'great game' in sign and I waved goodbye to Nandita.

'Goodbye, Dev, I've had a brilliant time.'

'What were you feeling sad about when I saw you

at the park, Cassia?'

I thought about Lula and Call-me-V, the way they looked at each other and what Dad had said about letting Lula be happy. And I thought about the big wave that had washed away Nandita's hearing, and the big hotel that would take away her game.

'Nothing, really. Well, nothing as important as this, anyway.'

'I am happy then. I did not like to see you looking so lost, London girl.' He stood and watched me as I turned to go.

I could still feel his eyes looking into mine, wide and brown, as I reached the house. I felt connected to something, something big and important, something that mattered. I didn't know what it was yet, but right now I thought I knew how Saachi felt.

Tea and Yams?

Priyanka and I hadn't spoken to each other since I tore up her sketch-book. Saachi and Lula tried to get us to make friends, but for ages Priya wouldn't even look at me. I knew she was upset about her pictures, but it didn't feel like it was totally my fault, not really.

In the end it was Granny-ji who got us all sorted out. She arrived one morning and announced, 'This is a thoroughly bad show and it cannot be going on any longer!'

When Saachi asked her what she had in mind she said, 'I am leaving it in the hands of the Gods.' Then Saachi said something about tea and yams and everyone else went, 'Aaah!'

It turned out the tea and yam thing was an ancient religious festival called a *Theyyam* that was held in the area every year. Saachi explained that during the ceremony different Gods and Goddesses, called Theyyams, entered the bodies of ordinary people.

The honour of being a Theyyam was passed down through families. Once they had put on the make-up and the costume, they sort of became the God or Goddess and you could ask them for help with problems in your life. Each Theyyam had a different main deity and some of them were super-powerful and a bit mean, so you had to be careful what you asked for.

On the way to the festival, I wondered which of my problems I should get the Goddess to help with. I had plenty to choose from, including how I was going to survive a day out with Princess Priya. We didn't say a word to each other in the car.

When Saachi drove away leaving me, Priya and Granny-ji standing silently at the side of the road, I realised it was going to be a very long day.

The festival had been going on since early that morning and now the food tent was dishing out bowls of steaming rice and vegetables to a hungry crowd. We took a plateful to Granny-ji, who was parked in a folding chair under a tree, and rejoined the end of the queue.

Priya handed me a cup of cool milky liquid. I must have looked a bit dubious because she said, 'Try it, Cassia. It is called curd-water and it is very good for keeping you hydrated.'

Was she talking to me again?

I took a big gulp of the sour salty drink, and whatever else Priya said was drowned out by my gagging noises. Obviously she was still working the hilarious practical jokes. I wished I'd stayed with Granny-ji, dozing under the trees.

By the time we reached the front of the dinner queue, my stomach was gurgling loudly. The days at Saachi's house had really given me a taste for Indian food, and as soon as we sat down I started shovelling spicy rice into my mouth with my fingers.

'I was going to say we have to hurry, Cassia, but I can see that is not necessary.' Priya's sarky tone made me feel like throwing my lunch at her.

She picked up our plates and threw them into the rubbish bin. I hoped the Theyyam would ignore whatever stupid stuff she wanted, but I still didn't know what I was going to ask for. Getting Lula away from Call-me-V and back to London was high on the list, and there was the hotel development too. For some reason, I was getting really bothered about that, bothered enough to push it up to the top of the list, maybe.

But what about me? If I could have just one chance to have something, then what should it be? And anyway, how would an Indian Goddess understand what a London girl wanted?

I tried to pretend Priyanka wasn't there while I watched one man prepare in a shady spot under the trees. He lay down on blankets on the ground while another man got busy with his make-up. This was a really important part of the ritual and the people watching stood by, respectful and quiet. Granny-ji had told me that this Theyyam was the Tiger Goddess, Puliyoor Kali, who had been born to the gods Lord Shiva and Parvathy when they'd gone walk-about in the forest.

Using a fine stick and pots of brightly coloured paste, a make-up man drew a swirly design which covered the performer's face and upper body. The background was orangey-gold, with thin lines and geometric shapes filled in with a glowing red colour. A thick circle of black outlined his eyes.

Once the make-up was finished, the Theyyam was helped into a costume of silver jewellery, and an amazing red-and-gold hooped skirt. Polished twists of silver, fixed behind his teeth, curled out of the sides of his mouth like tusks. Finally, a seriously blingo headdress was lifted on to his shoulders. Then the Theyyam picked up a small hand-mirror and stared intently into it.

Granny-ji had explained that when he opened his eyes wide, he would see the face of the Goddess staring back from the mirror so this was the moment he transformed and had the power to grant wishes and solve problems.

Even though I'd watched it all happen, it was more than someone putting on a costume, and I found I couldn't just stare at him like he was an actor or a dancer any more. He'd gone from an ordinary man to a Goddess.

The drumming signalled the Theyyam's arrival in the temple square and we scrambled to get a good place at the wall. Lots of the festival-goers seemed to have questions and problems. They came into the temple with offerings of money and the Goddess, surrounded by musicians and helpers, made slow, but dramatic, progress around the square. Everyone was a bit pushy, but we held on to our places.

The Goddess was getting closer and I still hadn't decided what to ask for. Possibilities flew through my mind, but nothing would stick in my head. I had seconds to decide. Granny-ji said you had to be careful what you wished for because it could really happen, but I didn't even know what I wanted!

The musicians were getting closer to where we were standing and I started to feel panicky. What if something really random and crazy came into my head as the Goddess passed, and it came true? Just thinking this cranked up my panic and my mind went into super-crazy mode. I had to get a grip.

I took a couple of deep breaths and tried to focus on what really mattered to me. What made me feel happy? Then I realised that what I really wanted was to have everything back the way it was before. I wanted to go back to when I was a girl who hung out in Camden Market, went to school and had a best friend who didn't hate her. Tears were starting to bubble up in my eyes. I tried hard to stop them before anyone saw.

I rubbed my eyes hard with my sleeve. Then I realised the Theyyam was standing right in front of me, staring unblinking into my face. I had the weirdest feeling that the Goddess could see right into my soul and that she knew what I wanted.

I started to feel really hot and dizzy. My mouth

was dry and I realised I could hardly speak. I swallowed a couple of times and managed to get out the words, 'I just want a friend.'

Everything got a bit weird and slo-mo then. I felt my legs go to jelly and I closed my eyes.

'Cassia!' Priyanka had hold of my arm and she was pulling me away from the temple wall. 'You looked really strange. People were staring at you.'

'Leave me alone, I'm fine! I just need a drink or something.'

Priyanka left me standing in the shade and fetched another cup of curd-water.

'Really? This is what you think I need?' I held my nose and swallowed the horrible drink. The taste hadn't changed but after a few mouthfuls it did make me feel a little better.

The Tiger Goddess had passed the spot where we'd been standing and the crowd had closed the gap, but I could still feel her eyes burning into my heart. I wondered what she had seen there – probably nothing very interesting. Why would she bother with my problems anyway?

After my moment at the temple wall, Priya said I should go and sit with Granny-ji for a bit and cool down. We still weren't talking much and I guessed she only wanted to make sure I didn't embarrass her again.

We had just wandered past a stand covered with strings of woven flowers and leaves when Priyanka grabbed my arm like a maniac. The bruises from my dramatic train rescue had only just stopped hurting and her nails dug into my wrists.

'By the temple pool. It cannot be true!' she shrieked.

'What? Where?'

'Jonny Gold!'

'Oh purlease!' I said sarcastically, but as I looked over to where Priya was pointing, I saw she was right.

Even with a baseball cap pulled down over his eyes, it was unmistakably him. He was moving away from us, so I set off at a run. I didn't know how Priya had spotted him, but this was my chance to meet Jonny Gold and I couldn't let her slow me down.

'He's heading for the taxis. We have to hurry!' I shouted. She still had hold of my arm and I was practically dragging her towards the road.

The Theyyam was getting busier and I struggled to make my way against the crowd. I quickly gave up on 'Excuse-mes' and barged my way through. I had shaken Priya loose and I was moving fast. I could just see Jonny's hat bobbing above the crowd and despite the crush of bodies, I seemed to be getting closer.

I looked around to check on Priya, who was making a high-pitched yelping sound like a crazy person, but when I turned back Jonny had disappeared into a surge of new arrivals. I jumped up and down, trying desperately to keep his hat in sight. Finally, I escaped out of the crowd just in time to see Jonny getting into a waiting car. I watched his tattooed arm, dangling out of the car window, as it disappeared into the distance.

Priya crashed into me and grabbed my wrist again. 'NOOOO!' we both wailed together and I realised we were hugging each other.

Lost in the craziness of actually seeing, then losing, Jonny Gold, neither of us said a word. Slowly, we made our way to where Granny-ji was sitting. We didn't bother fighting against the crowd any more either, we just let it push and pull us around like two beach balls bobbing on the tide.

'Was it really, really him?' Priya said.

She looked so serious I started to laugh. Then she started to laugh, too. We got louder and louder and more and more hysterical. People were beginning to stare. I got a stitch in my side and had to stop.

Granny-ji was awake when we finally reached her chair and she clapped her hands together as though she was really pleased to see us. I noticed Priya and I were walking with our arms linked together, just like friends out having a good time.

And it was true. Not-so-perfect Priya was a secret Jonny Gold grunge girl, and that meant we were bonded in fan-dom for ever.

Mangroves and Lily Pads

We got up late the next morning after an OMG-we-love-Jonny-Gold sesh that went on well past midnight. In the middle of the night, I'd remembered the newspaper with his picture on the front page, the one I'd bought during my choking fit in the shop.

I gave it to Priya to translate and she said it was a story about the golden one's new music video. Apparently he was looking for a paradise beach to use as a background and had decided Kerala was the perfect place to start looking.

'Can you imagine how amazing it would be if he came here?' Priya shrieked when she read it out. '*Amma* would have a nervous breakdown. She absolutely hates pop music and all those people tramping over her precious ecosystem. She'll go mad!'

I felt a bit uncomfortable hearing Priya talk about her mum like she was crazy. Loopy Lu was one thing, but Saachi was something else.

The last few days, Saachi had been really nice to me and told me lots about her research, which was not the yawn-fest I'd imagined. She'd defended exploited workers, stood up for women's rights and had even been arrested a couple of times. She talked to me about when she realised the law could help to change things and how important it was that people with big voices stood up for people whose voices didn't always get heard.

She said, 'Life isn't all *ha ha hee hee*, Cassia, but there is real joy in realising that everyone and everything is connected.'

Lula and Saachi met in England when they were students. They were eighteen years old and a long way from home. Lula was studying Design. She told me she'd said hello one morning at the library because Saachi looked so glamorous. It turned out that Saachi was looking for a flatmate and she was happy to share with Lula, even though she couldn't cook and was *really* untidy.

On Saturdays, Saachi searched the west end of the city for Keralan spices. Lula went with her and that was where her obsession with Indian fabrics started.

They explored the castles of Northumberland and Hadrian's Wall. Saachi laughed about the weather-related graffiti the Romans left behind and said she'd felt like adding a bit of her own. Lula made a full-length wool coat with an extra-thick lining for her. Saachi still has it hanging in the cupboard.

They took a market stall at the quayside on Sunday mornings and sold rice pancakes, cushion-covers and hand-made sweets to people strolling along the banks of the river Tyne. Saachi started doing free legal work for people and they marched in some political protests.

In those days Lula dressed a bit like a punk and Saachi was mostly in silk saree. They must have looked very odd together, waving placards about mining and nuclear weapons. Lula says that watching the film *Billy Elliot* always makes her cry because it reminds her of being young.

When it was time for them to go home, Lula was sad about the end of university, so Saachi invited her to come back to India. They used the money they had saved from the market stall to pay for an extra ticket. As Lula says, the rest is history, but I'm sure there's a lot she hasn't told me.

After breakfast Priya and I hung around the garden for a bit wondering what to do. She was all for going back to the Theyyam on a hunt for Jonny Gold, but Saachi asked if we could help the protest by taking photographs of the mangroves that lined the waterways and protected the land. Mangrove trees grew right into the water, perched up on their twisty roots as if they were on stilts.

Saachi explained that the mangrove trees sucked up salty sea-water through their drinking-straw roots, recycling it into fresh water that could be used in the village vegetable plots. Saachi wanted to record how many there were before the developers started chopping them down. She gave me her camera and we dragged a rowing boat down to the river.

Priyanka and I sat at either side of the boat, with an oar each. But right away she went into full princess mode and for a while we just splashed round in circles, laughing and getting wetter and wetter. When we did manage to go in a straightish line, Priya's oars got tangled up in weeds and lily pads and I was afraid we would capsize. In the end,

I suggested she should just read her magazine and leave the rowing to me.

It was hard work, but after a while I got into the rhythm of twist, dunk and pull on the oars and the boat slid gently through the water, leaving only shallow ripples behind. Further up from the riverbank, big brightly painted houses, like Priyanka's, sat partially hidden behind high walls.

Some of them were empty and they looked a bit bedraggled. I thought about taking photos of them for Lula, who liked that sort of thing, but I was on a mission for Saachi and I didn't know how long the batteries would last. So I rowed on. Priyanka said the owners were away, working, like her dad, in Dubai.

'I wish he wasn't so far away,' she said.

'Yeah, I know what you mean.'

'At least your dad lives in the same city.' She snapped the pages of her magazine.

'Does your dad come home often?'

'Not so often lately, but he sends me really nice presents.'

I slid the oars into the water again. 'What does he think about the hotel?'

'He says it is a good thing because it will bring money and jobs. He thinks *Amma* gets too sentimental about the village.'

Then she said she kind of agreed with her dad about the development. She thought it would be nice to have some good shops and maybe a few rich tourists around. She told me that her dad got cross with Saachi for getting involved in stuff that he said wasn't her problem.

'But it's good that she cares about people, isn't it?' I said.

She didn't reply and I wondered how you knew for sure when something wasn't your problem. The way Saachi talked about the environment seemed really personal, like she had decided one day to *make* it her problem no matter what anyone else thought. She was a bit like Dad – he made stuff his problem too. He got up a height about all kinds of things – mostly war, discrimination and people who didn't pick up their dog's poo.

I thought about them both, taking on the bad guys, like they were on a special mission to protect the world. Maybe one day I would be on a mission of my own. But what could I do? Perhaps recording the mangroves for Saachi was a good enough start. Tucking the oars into the side of the boat, I started taking the pictures she said she needed.

Priyanka dropped her magazine. It lay flapping in the bottom of the boat. Skinny models glowered from the glossy pages.

'They don't look like that in real life,' I said to her.

'What do you mean?'

'They mess around with the pictures to make the clothes look better. Dad says they should be ashamed of themselves... I was so jealous when I first met you, Priya.'

'Why?'

'I thought I'd be something special here, just because I was from London, and then it turned out you were waaay cooler than me.'

'Actually, I was also worried you'd be super-cool, just because you were from London. Imagine my disappointment!' she laughed.

'Oh very ha ha!' I splashed her with river water.

'I really wanted us to be best friends, Cass.'

She smiled at me and I realised my hands had stopped shaking. I picked up the camera and scanned the riverbank.

'Do you want to be a lawyer like your mum?' I asked Priyanka.

'Actually, I would really like to be involved in the

fashion industry.'

'Lula reckons London is the world fashion capital. She's been shoving brochures for design courses at me for ages,' I complained.

'I'd love to go to London, but I don't think my father would approve.'

'But Granny-ji is a big fan.'

'Granny-ji's never been! Her ideas about England all come from her old books. Once I heard her ask your *amma* how the London pea-soupers were these days.'

'What's a pea-souper?'

'I have no idea. Your *amma* just laughed and said they'd been blown away with the bowler hats.'

I stared across the river, shading my eyes from the glare of the water with Saachi's camera. While Priya talked about fashion, I snapped away until the low-battery light began to flash on the screen.

I picked up the oars and we splashed our way back to where the river joined the sea. I tied up the boat, and we went and sat on the beach. I checked the photos I'd taken. I hoped they were good enough. It looked like they were all in focus and I hoped Saachi would be pleased. I even managed to add the date and time to the album.

We swam for a bit, and then, after arranging to meet up later at the house, I left Priya on the beach with her magazine, and walked down the path which led to the netball court.

As I got closer, I hoped I would hear the shouts of a match going on, but there was no one around. A metal fence had been put up all around it and the gate was padlocked. The goal posts had already been sawn through ready for the bulldozers. They lay on the ground like felled trees, the ribbons on the hoops trailing on the dusty ground.

Seeing the empty court made me feel really sad for Nandita. I was glad I was doing something to stop the development now and I wondered when I'd see Dev again, so I could tell him.

Up on the hill, away from the beach, was the fencing which surrounded the new hotel development. A red truck was parked by the entrance gate. I wanted to get a few photos of the site for Saachi, so I turned off the path and started to follow the steep track upwards.

As I reached the top I heard voices coming from near the sign board. I couldn't understand the words, but one of the voices sounded familiar.

I suddenly felt really uncomfortable, like I was eavesdropping on someone I knew and it was too late to let them know I was there. I didn't want to be seen, so I ducked down behind the truck. The voices got louder and a man laughed. Now I was certain I knew his voice. Gravel crunched as the man walked away from me, and I stood up to get a better view.

Even from the back I recognised him.

It was Call-me-V.

He was holding a brochure with a picture of the new hotel on it and shaking hands with a man in a suit who seemed to be showing him around. Whatever Call-me-V had done, it had obviously made the man very happy. I ducked back down behind the truck.

What was Call-me-V doing here? Why was he being all buddy-buddy with the hotel developers? I knew he was a businessman like Priyanka's dad so maybe he thought the hotel was a good idea too.

I raised the camera to my face and zoomed in on the brochure and Call-me-V's head. His big cheating smile was in perfect focus. Seeing it super-sized, I felt furious. What a creepster, pretending all the time to be Saachi's friend. If Saachi found out she would go beyond Kali.

Then, with a rush of excitement, I realised I was right about him all along. Now all I needed to do was tell Lula and she would see him for the double-crossing stranger that he was and probably call off the wedding.

I pressed the green button and heard the camera whirr and click. It wasn't a loud noise but call-me-V looked across the bonnet of the truck and seemed to stare right at me. I felt my face flush and put the camera down.

Super-serious

There was no one at the house when I got back. I ran from room to room, looking for someone to tell my big news, but they were all empty and Saachi's car had gone, too. Even Priya had gone off without me.

I took a shower and then went to the kitchen and made myself a drink and a snack. It was weird being here alone. The house was quiet and every sound I made echoed in the empty rooms. I fetched my iPod, but the batteries were dead.

My Peacock book was lurking under a chair on the terrace. I had nothing else to do so I cracked it open again and caught up with the misery fest that was Una's life.

Her very wicked stepmother, Alix, was shopping in Paris and Una was off with her dad on an amazing sightseeing trip round India. But she wasn't having a good time and kept being sick. Una missed the poet boy too, but she didn't tell her dad about him.

I thought she should, just as I wished Lula had told me about Call-me-V. Secrets just got in the way and made stuff even harder. Then I remembered I hadn't told her about Rachel either. Maybe, like me, Lula just never found the right time.

'Oh, there you are. I've been looking for you for ages, Cass!' said Lula, appearing on the terrace. She sat cross-legged on the ground. All the spiky energy she'd been carrying around was gone. She looked really tired and a bit sad.

For a while Lula and I just sat staring out into the garden. She had stretched out her legs and her feet lay grilling in the sun. Her toes were already going pink. I realised I could tell her about Call-me-V now. Dish the dirt about him and the developers. Then she'd realise that he was the wrong person for her and start paying me a bit more attention.

'Mum, can I tell you something?'

'Of course, Cass, but do you mind if I go first?'

Typical, even when I found the right time to say something, it was wrong. I shrugged my shoulders and she took a deep breath, blowing the air out through her lips as though she was about to jump off a very high diving-board.

'The shop is in trouble, Cass, and I'm going to

have to close it down.'

'What?'

'I'm so sorry, Cass. It's been losing money for a while and Auntie Doré says the January sale has been a disaster. I've finally run out of time and money. I hate to do this, the shop means everything to me, and I know I've let you down, but I don't have any other choice.' She said it all in a rush as though she didn't dare to stop.

I couldn't believe what she was telling me. It had to be a mistake or some kind of horrible joke. I thought about our lovely shop. The way it smelled of incense and lemongrass. The rich colours of the cushions and rugs I lay on to play with my dolls when I was little. People's faces breaking into smiles when they walked through the door. It was our little palace and Lula was the queen bee. No wonder she'd been stressy.

'I thought the shop was doing really well... why didn't you tell me?'

'I didn't want to disappoint you, Cass. You like all your nice things.'

She was making it sound like it was partly my fault, that keeping the shop was done for me.

'What about our celebrity clients?'

'They've moved on to the next trend. I think

141

Mongolia is the new kid on the block now.'

'Can't Auntie Doré help?'

'She said she'd put money in, but only if I find a new range to sell.'

'What about Dad?'

'Your dad has his own life now. It's my shop. It's broken and I don't know how to fix it, but I won't ask your dad to throw his money away too.' She stared out into the garden and started twisting her earrings.

My head was still spinning, and I didn't really believe what Lula said could be true. But my body felt as if I'd been running downhill really fast. There was a panic feeling in my chest and my arms and legs were all shaky.

I took a couple of deep breaths. 'But how could you let this happen?'

'I'm sorry, Cass. I kept hoping things would change and they didn't and then it was too late.'

I didn't want to be angry with her, but I was. My whole life was going down the tubes and it was her fault. Mean, spiteful words jumped into my head and fizzed there. It would be so easy just to let them out, to blame her for everything.

Yet it wasn't really her fault. I knew how hard she worked and how much the shop meant to her. She didn't mean for it to turn out this way.

I looked at her hands twisting at her earrings and watched the expression on her face as she tried to pretend everything would be OK. I realised how much it must have cost to buy my plane ticket. She could have just left me with Dad, but she knew I was unhappy and lonely and so she brought me with her, even though it must have made her money troubles even worse. I felt a big wave of love surge up from my toes to the top of my head.

'Don't worry, Mum. You'll work it out and I'll help – I can stay off school for as long as you need me to.'

'Oh, Cass, that's a lovely offer, but you can't be on holiday forever.' She gave my hand a big squeeze.

A single tear had run down her face, following the smile lines at the side of her mouth, and now it was about to fall from her chin. I caught it with the tip of my finger. It shimmered in the sun and then dropped on to the floor.

'Please don't cry, Mum. You won't lose your shop, I promise.'

She wiped her eyes on her T-shirt and sniffed. 'I'm so sorry, Cass. I know you want to help and I love you for it, but I don't think there's anything anyone can do.'

'What does Call-me... I mean what does Mr Chaudhury say?'

'He says not to worry. It's just Karma, the good and bad things that I've done balancing themselves, and everything will work out in the end.'

'That's just stupid! There must be something we can do.'

'Well, we could stay here, Cass, with Vikram. It would be much sooner than I'd planned, but there are good schools and you could learn traditional Indian dancing.'

I really hoped she was joking, but she had her super-serious face on. It was worse than I thought. It wouldn't just be the shop I'd lose; it would be everything I knew.

I reached out for the camera. If I showed her the picture now, showed her Call-me-V hugging his brochure with his big bad buddy, we could go back to London, and then... what?

It was so complicated. Whatever I did, something would change. How could I decide? I stared at Lula hoping to find a clue in her face. But she just looked defeated. I was used to Lula fighting for stuff, but now it seemed like my poor mum had no punches left.

I remembered how happy she looked when she was with Call-me-V, all smiley and girlish. How she'd walked round the big shed, very serious, with a fan of incense sticks, waving perfumed smoke into the air.

I pushed the camera away again. There had to be a better way to do this, a way that wouldn't break her heart.

'Don't sell the shop, Mum, not yet. Wait, just for a bit.'

'I can't wait any longer, Cass, I've flapped around for too long already.'

'Please, Mum.'

'Why?'

'Maybe I can think of something.'

'There's nothing to be done, Cass.'

'Please!'

'All right. I won't do anything for a few more days, but Doré wants to get the estate agents on the case before I lose any more money.'

She stood up and wiped her eyes again and said she was going to her room to have a lie-down. The way she looked was scaring me. I didn't mind Lula acting a bit Loopy Lu, but really I expected her to be solid, dependable, sure of everything and able to sort out all our problems. Now I would have to help *her*.

But how? What could I do to make things right?

I sat on the terrace thinking about what had just happened. I remembered our first day here, Princess Priya, the banana trees, the killer wave and the music-filled party. It seemed like it had all happened a hundred years ago.

I felt tired and my arms were sore from the rowing. I lay back on the wooden floor, feeling the heat soak into my aching shoulders. I could hear the sea in the distance and slowly my eyes were starting to close. Maybe this was all just a terrible dream. I would wake up on the plane with Bollywood on the TV and drool on my chin.

Karma-cola

I thought at first the shaking ground was in my imagination, but when I opened my eyes I saw that the terrace was definitely vibrating. Was it an earthquake?

I sat up just as Priya hurled herself across the floor and landed at my feet. She was panting hard, but still trying to speak. 'It's him!' she shrieked, finally managing to communicate something I could sort of understand. 'He's coming here, he's actually coming here in actual real life!'

'Who? And please stop yelling, Priya. Seriously, I'm having the worst day ever and you're making my ears bleed!'

'Him! Jonny Gold! He's found his dream beach and it is this one. You're wrong, Cassia, you're not having the worst day ever, this must actually be the best day of our lives.'

When Priyanka finally calmed down, she

explained that Jonny Gold's record label had chosen our beach to film his new song. Then I knew I must be dreaming. Perhaps a coconut had landed on my head and I was concussed, or maybe it was Priya who'd been hit on the head – she was raving enough for both of us.

I must have been giving her a proper 'Yeah, right!' look because she dragged me back into the house and barged into Saachi's office.

Saachi was talking to someone on the phone. She looked a bit cross and parked the receiver back with a thunk as Priya launched herself into 'She-doesn't-believe-me-but-it's-true-Amma-isn't-it?'

Saachi snorted and said, 'Om Shanti, my eye!' and that yes, it was true, but she couldn't imagine why anyone would be happy to have the honky-tonky circus coming to town and why didn't we go away and find something useful to do?

Priya dragged me back into the garden and we headed for the hammock. She was practically hyperventilating with excitement and I was glad when she sat down. She swung her legs over the side of hammock and gave the ground a shove with her feet.

'We have to get him to notice us, Cassia! We have

to get on TV!'

'Agreed, but what did you have in mind, besides super-loud squealing, of course?'

'Aren't you the one who's the dancing queen?'

'Well, yes, but…'

'No buts, this is serious business! You have to get some kind of dance routine together so I can make the costumes and then we can show Jonny Gold when he comes to the beach, and he will see that I am super-talented, and *Amma* and Daddy-ji will understand that being in fashion has good earning potential and let me go to college in London.'

She gave the ground another hard shove and the hammock swung wildly over the flower bed. She had it all worked out, and I had to admit it was a killer idea. Not just for her, but for me too. If I could get on to Jonny Gold's video, show him what a brilliant dancer I was, then he'd probably want me to be in all his music videos, pay me loads to choreograph and even tour with the band. And I could talk to him about the hotel.

He would hate the idea of the development, his lyrics were so spiritual he was bound to be an eco-freak like Saachi. And because he was such an important person he would be able to stop the hotel being built.

Then I could tell Lula and Saachi about Call-me-V and his sneaky investments and Saachi would chase him back to Kochi. And Jonny would be so happy with my dancing he'd buy loads of stuff from the shop and Lula would be able to keep it open after all, and she'd be so happy she'd hardly notice Call-me-V had gone and we could all hang out together in London. It was perfect, utterly perfect!

A fly landed on my arm. I looked down to swat it away and saw that the swirly *mehandi* tattoo Mrs Chaudhury had painted on my hand was almost completely faded. She had told me to be careful what I wished for, but this was a real wish come true and nothing could go wrong.

'All right, Priya, let's get started. First we need some music!'

'No, first we need some outfits!' She swung out of the hammock and jogged back to the house, shouting, 'Come on, Cassia, hurry up!'

Priya was on a life-changing mission and it was all a bit scary. How was she so sure of what she wanted? Maybe big ambition ran in her family. Whatever, I was happy to get carried along by her unstoppable energy. I struggled to escape from the folds of hammock which had wrapped me up like a banana skin and followed her up the stairs.

When I got to her room, she was already throwing great heaps of clothes on to her bed and muttering. It seemed safer to stay out of the way, but she pulled me back into the middle of the room and flashed one top after another under my chin. They all looked good enough to me, but within a few minutes she had three piles heaped on the bed.

As each outfit was tested she stared for half a second then barked 'Yes!', 'No!', or 'Maybe', which decided which pile it joined. Just as I thought I was going to faint with all the stand-still-and-stand-up-straight stuff, Priya finally announced that she was satisfied and what did I think?

She propelled me towards the opposite wall. I looked at myself in the mirror. The bluey-green silk was the same colour she'd chosen for me for the bridesmaid's dress, the one I'd seen in the sketch-pad and ripped up in a fit of jealous temper. The fabric, edged with gold, bounced light on to my face making my skin look caramel-creamy, instead of the pale freckled wreck I was used to seeing. It made my eyes look bigger too, and the mass of frizzy curls I so hated glowed around my head.

My lips widened as I smiled at myself. Priya had loaded my arms with bracelets from an overflowing jewellery box and now she was stitching a patterned scarf to the bottom of my jeans.

'This outfit is totally amazing, Priya!'

'Fusion clothes for a fusion girl. You know you are actually *very* 21st century, Cassia.' She was busy changing into a version of my outfit in pink and gold. Standing side by side we looked like an advert for toothpaste and global harmony.

I went to my case and took out the present I had bought for her in London. 'Here, Priya, I hope you like them,' I said.

She unwrapped the tissue paper and I watched her face break into a huge smile as she slid the bracelets over her arm. '*Very* urban cool, Cass! How did you guess this is exactly my style?'

I muttered something about Top Shop and she gave me a hug. I found the scented oil Mrs Jaffrey had given me in Kochi and splashed it on our outfits. The room filled up with the smell of flowers.

'That smells delicious!' Priya said. 'Come on, Cass, it's time to teach me how to dance!' She snapped the lid of her laptop open and pushed it towards me.

Looking at her Jonny Gold playlist, I realised that, compared with Priya, I was just an amateur. She had everything downloaded, absolutely *everything*, including some mixes I'd never heard. She plugged in a couple of speakers and Jonny Gold's beautiful voice came pouring into the room like runny honey.

I lifted my arms up high above my head, ready to start dancing, and the bangles tinkled as they cascaded down from my wrists. The Golden One had only got to the first chorus of *Galloping Soul* when Saachi came blasting in after him.

'Girls, you really need to keep the noise down. I'm trying to work, you know.'

'But it's Jonny Gold, *Amma!*'

'Well, please take Mr Karma Cola and his music somewhere else.'

'But we need to dance!'

'Cassia, I was hoping you had some time to help me, as a matter of fact. Your photos of the mangroves were excellent and now it is important to catalogue them properly so they can be used as evidence.'

I wanted to say yes, but before I had a chance Priya jumped up.

'She can't help you, *Amma*. She's helping me!'

'I don't understand,' Saachi said.

So Priya explained our plan to her, how getting on the video would help to stop the hotel.

Saachi looked a bit sceptical and I realised I would have to choose between dancing with Priya and working with Saachi. I really wanted to do both, but there wasn't enough time.

'Could I help with the cataloguing tomorrow?'

'OK, if you really need to practise now, go to Vikram's workshop. The electricity is on and I'm sure he won't mind.'

I was about to argue – I really didn't want to bump into Call-me-Sneaky today, but Priya had already scooped up her laptop and was shoving me towards the door.

There was a breeze scudding up from the beach and our scarves twirled to escape, kite-like, into the sky. I thought our costumes looked a bit stagey for a normal day. But I saw how people looked at us and smiled. Priya obviously had a talent for this whole dressing-up thing.

She talked non-stop all the way up the road

about how she really wanted to do fashion and how she'd had to keep it secret from her mum and dad because it wasn't a serious enough career for them. She'd worked extra hard at school so they couldn't accuse her of wasting time reading magazines and shopping.

In Dubai, with her dad, she raked through every designer shop in the city, noticing what had sold well and what was still dragging on the rails. She'd search out vintage stuff online, too. She'd shown me a tailored wool jacket with huge shoulder pads that Lula had brought over for her on last year's buying trip. I remembered it hanging in our wardrobe for ages. Priya had taken it apart like a clothes surgeon. She stripped it down to the skeleton, exposing the guts so she could see how it was put together.

For Priya, fashion wasn't just frocks, it was practically a science project and I recognised that same obsessive head that Lula got when she was looking at fabric. I felt a twinge of jealousy. Maybe Priya should be the one to help save the shop. She probably had loads of good ideas and Lula obviously loved her.

Then I remembered Priya was my friend. It wasn't a competition. She cared about Lula and about me.

She didn't think I was a big-mouth loser, which was what Rachel thought. The dresses she'd designed for the wedding were beautiful, especially mine.

'I'm sorry I ripped up your sketch-books, Priya.'

'It's OK. Now we're friends, I can do something even better!'

It turned out there was a major flaw in our brilliant plan to impress Jonny Gold with our talents – and the flaw was Priya.

I showed her all my best moves, but she just didn't get it. She looked pained by my choreography, as though she was fighting, not dancing.

'Priya! I thought you liked Jonny Gold!'

'I love him! I just can't move like that!'

'Look, just watch me and do *exactly* what I do!' I begged her for what felt like the zillionth time.

I swung into the sequence again. Losing my balance a little in the middle didn't matter because I just added an extra jump and a side step.

'I am doing *exactly* what you do, but you keep changing it!'

'It's not a change, it's just a bit of improvisation.'

'But how can I follow you if you are making it up?'

'How can you be so utterly rubbish at this? I thought all Indian girls were genetically graceful. Just let your body follow the music!'

'I can't! That jumpy jerking isn't what my body hears!' She looked as though she was about to cry.

'Please, try again Priya, you're doing really well.'

'You just said I was utterly rubbish!' She sat down.

'I didn't really mean it, honestly.' It was a lie but I couldn't let her give up now – I needed a dance partner. 'Priya, get up. I'll stop shouting, I promise.'

'OK, but this is the last time, my feet really hurt. Actually, my everything really hurts.'

I heard the workshop door open and guessed Call-me-V had arrived. I wouldn't be able to dance while he was lurking. Why did he have to come in and spoil everything? Wasn't it enough that he was involved in the development and lying to Saachi? The door creaked shut again.

Had Call-me-V been spying on us? I felt a shiver of fury go up my spine and I turned round. The bright sunlight streaming through the open door kept the figure in silhouette, making it hard to see. There were two figures in the doorway now.

The taller one stepped into the light and my heart skipped a beat or three.

'Hello again, London girl, what kind of trouble are you in today?'

Timepass Things

Nandita came in behind Dev, waved to me and settled herself on one of the workbenches. I cued the music and counted Priya in. They both watched us begin the routine without saying anything.

It started off all right, but after the first chorus I was in deep despair. Nandita giggled as Priya flapped around, biting her bottom lip in fierce concentration. I felt strange with Dev watching, and I realised my body had gone a bit awkward and off the beat, too.

I knew Nandita couldn't hear the music, so I was really surprised when, halfway through the second verse, she jumped up and stood facing me and started mirroring every step and twist I took.

She seemed to have a way of watching me and moving her own body all at the same time, like there was a perfect pathway between her brain and her feet. Perhaps it was the signing that had trained her to know what her body was doing without checking.

I didn't know for sure how she did it, but whatever special powers she was calling on, she could dance Priya into the cheap seats. I was feeling some serious pressure too.

The track came to an end and Priya flopped down on the ground. I was about to do the same, when I realised Nandita was still dancing. The music had stopped, so she must have had a soundtrack in her head that was driving her movements. But they weren't anything I'd shown her. She reminded me of the Kathakali actors we'd seen in Kochi, because Nandita wasn't just dancing, she was story telling.

I'd never watched dancing without music before and in the beginning it looked strange. I knew Dev and Priya were still in the room and I knew that there was a busy village on the other side of the wooden doors, but the only sounds I heard were Nandita's feet scuffing puffs of dust up from the dirt floor. No wonder she was so brilliant at netball. She'd move furiously fast, then stop and hold a pose until her muscles must have been screaming.

At home I swaggered and clowned to my favourite tracks because it made me feel different, special – I could lose ordinary Cassia in a fantasy of glamour and fame. But it looked like Nandita danced to be more real, not to escape into dreams but to escape from them. I could see that she was a dancer, a proper dancer. When I danced I was having a good time, but compared with Nandita, I was just playing at dance. What was it Dev had said about 'timepass things' and things that really mattered?

As I watched her, I realised that Nandita was like Rachel. When she was dancing, Rachel had the same look of total concentration I could see now on Nandita's face. No wonder my mucking about frustrated her, and it explained why she was so upset with me that day at the rehearsals. Remembering Rachel's angry words, and what I had done next, I felt ashamed.

She was right. If I couldn't respect the dance and the other dancers then I didn't deserve to be in the group. I thought chucking me out meant she wasn't my friend, but maybe it was my own fault.

Finally, Nandita stopped dancing and did a very serious *Namaste* bow, which I returned.

Priya was whooping and clapping madly, and over the noise I shouted, 'Dev, how do you sign *That was amazingly incredible*?' Then, without waiting for an answer, I gave Nandita a huge hug and nearly lifted her off her feet.

Dev had been doing something on Priya's computer and I saw him look up and smile at his sister in a way that made my already-racing heart bang in my chest.

Priyanka was making it's-snack-time noises, but I wanted to keep practising so I pretended I couldn't hear her and went to see what Dev was doing.

I guessed Nandita was hungry too because, with a bang of the door, she and Priya were gone and it was just me and Dev. It seemed suddenly to have got loads hotter in the room. I thought I should say something, but I had no idea what.

'Your sister is a brilliant dancer.'

Dev didn't answer. He was doing something on Priya's computer and the tapping of the keyboard sounded unnaturally loud. I wiped a trickle of sweat out of my eye.

Finally Dev looked up from the screen, pressed *Enter* and said, 'What do you think of this, London girl?'

A tune started to drift out of the speakers. I couldn't make it out at first. It sounded like Jonny Gold's new track *Om Shanti, Babe* but there was another beat running underneath it, just nudging the music towards something real, something more exciting.

As the song went on, the Indian beat got stronger and Jonny's voice gently faded into the background. Then the music became more melodic, more Indian and I could hear sitars and drums. And now Jonny was back, his voice drifting in and out of the rhythms with a cool London feel.

'How did you do that?' I said, looking over his shoulder at the virtual mixing desk he'd dug out of Priya's laptop.

'I told you I liked computers and your friend has a lot of music in here.' He patted the machine like it was a puppy who'd done a clever trick.

'You made it sound much more Indian.'

'It *should* sound properly Indian – the track is called *Om Shanti, Babe*, after all!'

'What does *Om Shanti* actually mean?'

'*Om* is the sound of the universe and *Shanti* means peace. It can be said as a way of wishing well to someone you care about.' He smiled at me.

'This will be perfect for Nandita! Do you think she'd like to dance with us?'

'She will like that very much.'

'But how will you explain the tune to her?'

'If the music is loud enough, Nandi can feel the rhythm and also I will show her. I can dance too,

London girl.'

Then he put on something slow and dreamy and held out his hand for me. I stood up and tried to remember some of Nandita's graceful moves, but after a couple of steps I realised this was just Saturday night dancing, and it was great. We'd nearly got to the end of the track when, with a dying groan, the music stopped and all the lights went out.

In the sudden silence I felt Dev's hand brushing mine. He was standing very close to me and I could feel his warm breath on my neck. His hand touched my shoulder and then his lips were very close to mine, too.

'Cassia, I wish to kiss you. Will this be all right?'

Surprised, I pulled back a little and felt his hand drop away. I reached out for it in the darkness, feeling his cool skin and smooth finger-nails. My skin went goosebumpy, the hairs standing on end and sending shivers into my spine. I absolutely definitely did want to kiss him, but it had to be a proper kiss, no crashing teeth, nothing bitey, or grabby, or slobbery that might spoil this utterly perfect moment.

'Cassia?' he said.

'Um, sorry, I think that would be all right... I mean, yes.'

And moving towards each other very slowly, carefully avoiding bumping noses, we kissed. And it was perfect, gentle, and exciting and totally amazing.

Smiling and holding hands in the dark, I realised Priya was right. This was the strangest, most unexpected and without a doubt the very, very best day of my life.

Gilded Bears

It seemed as if a hundred years had passed before Priya and Nandita came crashing back into the workshop with a bag full of food and bottles of water.

The electricity was still off, but we hunted around the cupboards, still full of the old pans and candle-making equipment, until we found some samples left over from when Call-me-V's shed was a proper workshop. The wicks were dry and dusty, but they lit easily enough and the golden-coloured pools of light gave the space the feeling of a stage set.

Priya said it was as if Diwali, the festival of light, had come round again. She said Granny-ji remembered when the workshop had been a good business, employing a lot of local people. They had produced handmade beeswax candles that were well known for burning with a strong, clear light that lasted for ages.

The workshop slowly filled up with the faint smell

of honey, smoking up from the melting beeswax, and reminding me of Auntie Doré's super-swishy dining room decorated with perfumed candles.

We washed our hands and then all sat down together and unpacked the food. As we ate, I told Priya about how Dev had saved me from certain death in the train. I might have made it sound a bit too dramatic because Priya looked at Dev like he was a superhero.

It was weird acting all normal after me and Dev had kissed. I wanted to sit close to him, but since Priya and Nandita had come back I felt stupidly self-conscious. I kept remembering the feel of his lips on mine and realised I was smiling like an idiot. I hoped he felt the same.

I thought Nandita must have noticed something because she kept staring at Dev, and he kept avoiding her eyes. Luckily, she was practically bursting with questions about Jonny Gold.

With Dev signing, I explained about using the dance routine to get Jonny to notice us, and how we thought he'd be so impressed he'd listen to our story about the hotel. It would be brilliant to get such an important person on our side.

While Priya was doing her designer bit on our

costumes back at the house, I'd made some notes about the plan and now I pulled them out of my pocket. I realised now that Nandita should be the star, not me - she was a much better dancer and I knew that Jonny Gold would be really impressed by her.

I said that we'd have to pick a spot on the beach where he'd be able to see us. Then we could start the music and just let our perfect plan play out. I had a list of things we needed to do and, while everyone was eating, I read it out.

I got a round of applause when I'd finished, just like Saachi at the party when she'd explained about the hotel development to the villagers. Dev smiled at me and Nandita gave me a thumbs-up sign. I realised I'd got them all organised and committed, and that meant I must be pretty good at this stuff. Priya started planning a make-over for Nandita. It was so good to be in a gang of friends again.

We finished eating and Dev cued up the music. Maybe it was following Nandita, or all of us dancing together, but something had inspired Priya and she was keeping time at last. We went through it a zillion times, with Dev making adjustments to the music as we worked on the routine.

It was turning into a kind of musical play about

squabbling sisters all in love with the same boy. Nandita was the star and we each had different styles of dancing. Dev signalled the changes to Nandita, counting out the beats in sign.

We had it almost perfect when the big wooden doors opened. I was hoping to see Saachi or Lula coming through the door, but it was Call-me-V, jangling the keys.

'I hope the workshop has been a good place for you, but it is time to be going home now.'

'Already!' wailed Priya.

'It is actually quite late, Priyanka.'

Trust him to come and spoil our fun, I thought. I started blowing out the candles. Dev and Nandita were already heading for the door and I realised I didn't even know where they lived.

As I reached them, Call-me-V stepped in front of me. 'Cassia, I am very happy to see you are making new friends here.' I wanted to get outside, but Call-me-V was determined to get into a conversation. 'So, where did you meet these young people?'

Why was Call-me-V being so nosy about Dev and Nandita? What did my friends have to do with him? I pushed passed him trying to get outside as fast as I could. I wanted to say goodbye to Dev properly, but it was too late. When I looked around, the road outside was empty. We hadn't even organised when we would meet again. Why was Call-me-V always in the way, interfering in my life?

Priya came out of the shed and linked arms with me and we hurried down the hill back to the house.

Saachi and Lula were waiting in the living room when we got back. They both had their serious faces on and Lula was twisting her earrings manically. It wasn't that late and they knew where we'd been, but still I wondered if we were in trouble. The rest obviously hadn't done Lula much good.

'*Amma*! We have to keep practising. You should see us all dancing, it is amazing!'

'Calm down, Priya. You must please stop shouting and listen. This is important and not easy to say.' She took a big swallow of water and cleared her throat. 'I have found out who owns Auramy Incorporated. I had my suspicions confirmed today at the law firm in Kannur. As a matter of fact, the clue was in their name, Auramy. It's Latin, but until I had some spying done and remembered the graffiti about the bears that Cassia noticed, I couldn't make the connection.'

I didn't know what she was getting at, but I could see by Priyanka's expression that she was at least one step ahead of me and it wasn't good news.

Saachi looked very uncomfortable. 'Auramy is another word for gold. The company is registered to something called Gilded Bear Records in London. I'm so sorry, girls, I really am, but it's your Jonny Gold who is behind the hotel development.'

'That isn't true!' I protested. 'He only found the perfect beach for his video a few days ago.'

'Cassia, I think the story in the newspaper was just a publicity stunt.'

'I don't understand.'

'It's not really a video for his new song, it's more of an advert for his new hotel. People will see the beach and want to visit it. Having his own hotel here means he will make money out of fans and tourists.'

'But he's really into the environment, *Amma*. His lyrics are all about love and nature. It can't be him!' said Priya, shaking her head.

'I know you don't want to believe me, but I have seen the evidence. There is no doubt in my mind.

Jonny Gold and his record label are the ones building the hotel.'

I sat very still for a minute, and then I felt our dance-practice picnic rising back up my throat. There was a very good chance I was going to throw up. When I thought of all our plans to impress him with our dancing in order to get him on our side about the development, my stomach squeezed into a tight ball. I thought Jonny Gold was going to be the one to help us, and all the time he was the one we had to stop.

I heard someone shout, 'No!' and realised it was me. I ran out of the room and slammed the door so hard that a chunk of plaster fell off the wall. It landed on the tiles with a sharp crack and a puff of chalky dust rose up from the floor. The stillness of the garden swallowed me up for a while, and all I could hear was my own jagged breathing.

Then, from the house, Saachi's voice cut into the night air. The veranda light clicked on and I saw her silhouette gliding purposefully across the grass towards me. 'Cassia, I'm so sorry.'

'You're wrong,' I yelled back. 'You must have made a mistake!'

'There is no mistake, I'm afraid.'

'It can't be him, Saachi, it just *can't*!'

'Oh, Cassia, I know it's hard when your heroes let you down.'

'I want to go home!' I cried and the tears started gushing, and my nose began to run, and my mouth got tight and watery. She hugged me as I blubbed and howled until my chest hurt.

Suddenly, barking echoed from somewhere in the dark and I felt her laugh.

'I'm sorry, Cassia. I know it's not funny, but you've set the tree-foxes off.'

I rubbed my face on her soft shawl. 'I'm sorry I shouted at you.'

'Don't worry, you had a lot to shout about.'

'How am I going to tell Dev and Nandita? They'll be so disappointed.'

'This isn't your fault, Cassia. You were trying to do a good thing. You could all still dance, you know. I'd understand. The hotel development isn't really your battle to fight.'

'But it feels like it is now,' I said. And then I explained about promising to save the netball court for Nandita and her friends, and how I wanted to do something which mattered to other people, just like her.

'Well, so long as you understand taking on the world will make your life a lot more complicated, Cassia.'

Suddenly I found myself blurting out, 'Priya doesn't want to be a lawyer, you know.'

'I am not surprised. Mums are a hard act to follow.'

'Lula will look after her if she comes to London to study fashion.'

'I know. Luella is my best friend. I've always thought of her as Priya's second mother, and I am so glad to have met *you*, at last.'

Talking to Saachi was different from talking to Lula or Dad and I knew I could tell her things that were difficult to share with them. I really wanted to tell her the whole story about Rachel and me. It was like a bad tooth that wouldn't stop hurting until it was taken out.

'Saachi, I was angry with my best friend, Rachel, and I messed up our chances in a big dance competition. She said I didn't take things seriously enough and that she would never speak to me again.'

'You seem to be a very serious person to me, Cassia.'

'I didn't realise how hard she worked to get the routines right and how much it mattered to her until it was too late.'

'Is it too late?'

'Yes. The competition's over, I forgot to bring the proper music and we had to make do with what they had. It made us look like we couldn't be bothered. I ruined everything.'

'There will be other competitions, other chances, you know.'

'But Rachel will never let me back in the group.'

'Tell her how sorry you are, Cassia, and show her that you mean it. She is probably missing you, too.'

'It doesn't feel like it now.'

'I know, but that will change, I'm sure of it.' She smiled and gave me a hug.

It felt so good to have finally told someone, someone who understood how bad I'd been feeling. The relief was so huge I started to laugh, getting louder and louder, until the gulps and hiccups turned into crying again.

Saachi stayed with me, gently stroking my head, until I was all cried out. Then she went back into the house and a few minutes later Priya came and sat with me. I saw she'd been crying too.

'Don't be sad, Priya.'

'But I can never listen to Jonny Gold's songs ever again!'

'Yes, you can. He may be a greedy, lying creepster, but he can still sing.'

Bath-time for Baby

The next morning, after a rather gloomy breakfast, Priya set off for school, grumbling all the way up the road. It was a cloudy day but still really hot, and the lack of air made me feel flat and cranky. Lula hadn't even got up yet and Saachi said I should let her sleep as she had a lot on her mind. She wasn't the only one, I thought.

There was no point trying to find Dev and Nandita and I didn't want to just hang about all by myself. So, when Saachi suggested a trip into the hills, I thought it would be a really good chance to talk to her about Call-me-V, among other things.

I went upstairs and put on a sweater and jeans because she said it could get chilly once we got high into the forest. As I opened the wardrobe the smell of the perfumed oil from our costumes drifted out. I fetched the little bottle Mrs Jaffrey had made for me back in Kochi, twisted open the tasselled top, tipped a couple of drops on to my hand and breathed in the flowery smell.

Outside on the veranda, I saw Call-me-V reversing the Green Goddess down the drive, and I guessed he was moving it away so Saachi's car could get past.

He wound down the window and waved to me from the driver's seat. 'Jump in, Cassia, we have a long drive ahead of us.'

What did he mean, "we"? Then Saachi came out of the house, looking harassed, and said she had been called into a meeting about the development and I would have to go without her.

My face must have twisted because she squeezed my hand and said quietly, 'Vikram is a great guide, Cassia. You will learn a lot and I'm sure you will enjoy each other's company, if you give yourselves a chance.'

I turned to walk back to the house, but Saachi touched me on the elbow and I stopped.

'Do this for your mother, Cass. It is so important to her that you at least try to get along with Vikram. He is a good man and he makes Luella very happy.'

Call-me-V smiled and opened the passenger door. 'I thought we could start with a visit to the elephants. Does that sound good, m'n?'

'I suppose so.'

I climbed into the car and Saachi loaded a couple of tiffin tins on to the back seat.

We left the village and, using the back roads, we climbed into the hills. We sat in complete silence for ages, but as soon as we reached the forest, Call-me-V went into teacher mode, pointing out sites of environmental interest and birds of prey until, in desperation, I asked him to switch on the radio. When he hummed along to a few of the songs, I closed my eyes, hoping I could shut him out and shut him up for ever.

'Cassia, you have something bothering your mind. I would very much like to know what it is.'

I opened the window wider. The warm air rushed over my face, making my ears pop.

'Cassia, please do not stick your head out of the window. It is very dangerous; stones may fly up in your eyes.'

Now he sounded like my dad, seeing disaster around every corner. How dare he act like my dad! Dad was one of the good guys, not like Call-me-Creepy.

'I saw you at the hotel site, doing deals with the developers,' I blurted out.

'Ah yes! That was very good fun.'

'Fun? Do Mum and Saachi know?'

'Actually, it was Saachi's idea. Mostly she is a very sensible lawyer, but every now and then she has an attack of the Secret Sevens. I can only imagine this is what happens when you are raised in a house full of old English children's books.'

'You mean you weren't investing in the hotel?'

'Oh no, but they believed I was a rich man from Dubai.'

'You were spying on them!'

'Oh, yes, I wanted to wear a false moustache, but your mother and Saachi would not hear of it.'

'So was it you who found out about Jonny Gold?'

'I learned just enough for Saachi to put the pieces together.'

I didn't know what to say. I felt really embarrassed. I'd thought he was deceiving everyone, but really he'd been helping all the time.

'Are you angry that your Mr Gold was not who you expected, Cassia?'

I thought about Jonny Gold's songs about rainforests and icebergs, and the things he said in interviews about the environment. I wondered if he meant any of it, or if it was all just a publicity stunt.

Jonny must have known about the protest, but he didn't seem to care. Maybe he should have listened to his own lyrics because, it seemed to me, that Jonny had galloped away from his soul somewhere along the way.

'No, not angry exactly, I feel a bit stupid, that's all. And it makes me want to stop the hotel even more.'

'If you are serious about helping Saachi, Cassia, then perhaps we should do more than just visit the elephants. We should ask for some help.' He stroked the stone statue sitting on the dashboard, and at the next junction he turned the car up a narrow track which led into the forest.

He pulled up outside the elephant reserve and found a place to park. We unloaded the picnic and sat on a patch of grass in the shade. While I was setting out the food on a rug, Call-me-V told me about the Hindu Elephant God, Ganesh. He said that Ganesh rode around on a tiny mouse to show how you should keep your ego small and not let your own sense of importance boss you around. Ganesh was like the patron saint of business people and writers.

But the really big thing about Ganesh was that he was in charge of making and getting rid of problems. He even had a special crook like Little-Bo-Peep, to hook away bad *karma*. He explained that *karma* is actions, the stuff you do that brings rewards and punishment. I laughed when he told me that Ganesh's belly was so big because it held the past, the present and the future, like eggs, inside it.

'I have no such excuse, Cassia,' Call-me-V said, rubbing his own stomach. 'My build is on the healthy side, but the reasons are laid out on the tablecloth, as you can see!'

'Would Ganesh help me, even though I'm not a Hindu, or even from India?'

'Ganesh has travelled around the world for over 2000 years; I'm sure if you are asking nicely he will at least listen.'

I wondered if it was really that simple, that you found the right god and then asked them to sort things out. Even if it wasn't the way it really worked, I liked the idea that that you could put stuff that bothered you into a question. Maybe making it a saying-it-out-loud thing was the first step to changing things yourself.

We finished eating, tidied up the picnic and went into the elephant reserve. We'd arrived at bath-time and, lying on her side in a pool, was a baby elephant.

She slapped her trunk from side to side, spraying

water into the air. She looked like a guest at an elephant health club. The Mahout, who looked after the elephants, was using a coconut shell to scoop water on to her back. He greeted Call-me-V, then handed me a lump of coconut husk.

'It is a privilege to wash an elephant, Cassia. They are sacred animals, so make the most of it,' Call-me-V said.

Feeling very honoured, I greeted the baby elephant and did the hands-pressed-together bow as a sign of respect. Then I rolled up my jeans and waded into the warm muddy water. Dunking the brush in the bath, I started scrubbing at the baby's leathery skin. Clumps of dark hairs sprouted out of her back. I touched one with the tip of my finger.

The elephant's body was warm and I could feel her chest expanding under my hands, as she sighed and snorted with pleasure. I scrubbed the crease behind her ears and she nuzzled my arm with her trunk.

'She is liking you,' said the Mahout, smiling.

'What is not to like? This is a very promising young person. She cares about her family and her friends, other people and the environment,' Call-me-V said, smiling, as though he was proud of me.

I felt strange hearing him say nice things about

me, especially after I'd been so suspicious of him.

'Yes, I have heard from Saachi how you are helping her. She told your mother you have the makings of a very good lawyer,' he said.

Saachi thought I had talent! I felt my face go red. I stroked the baby elephant's head and she reached her trunk up to my face. I'd thought everything in my life was going wrong, but maybe Ganesh had put some good *karma* my way after all.

We stayed until the baby elephant was done with her bath, then Call-me-V fired up the Green Goddess and we lurched and bumped our way further up into the hills.

After a long steep climb, Call-me-V stopped the car at a small tribal settlement. A man in a checked cloth, folded up into shorts, that Call-me-V said was called a *dhoti*, came out to meet us. They talked together for a bit and then Call-me-V asked if I wanted to see the way wild honey was collected. He got a glass jar out of the Goddess's boot and we walked up a narrow, tree-lined path.

We were going to a nest they already knew about, but Call-me-V explained that when they were hunting for new nests, the honey-gatherers would sometimes follow forest birds, who led them to the right place.

They rewarded the birds with a bit of the honey in case they took revenge the next time, and led them to a snake's nest instead.

The honey man, Mr Kumaran, stopped and pointed at a bamboo ladder leaning against a tall tree. High up, I could see an oval-shaped lump wedged into the cleft of a hollow branch. Mr Kumaran gathered a handful of dried leaves, tied them together with string and started a smoky fire going. The pale grey curls drifted up towards the honey-comb.

'The smoke makes the bees drowsy, so they will not be so quick to sting us.' Call-me-V explained. Mr Kumaran climbed up the ladder, and carefully cut a small chunk of the honey-comb, leaving the rest of the nest. Bees started to fly around our heads and we moved away, slowly. A bee settled on my hand. I was about to brush it off when Call-me-V stopped me.

'If it breaks its sting, it will die. Just keep very still, Cassia, and let it fly away.'

Mr Kumaran put the lump of honey-comb into a cloth and held it over the jar. Then he squeezed the cloth in his hands. Golden honey oozed out of the comb and ran over his fingers before drizzling down the neck of the jar. He dribbled a taste on my hand, too. It was delicious, strong and sweet. When there was no more honey left to press, Call-me-V put a lid on the jar and we started the long walk back to the Green Goddess.

'What happens to the left-over wax when all the honey has been squeezed out?' I said.

'It can be used for many things, like medicine, cosmetics, and of course, candles. But unless it can fetch a fair price, much of it is wasted,' Call-me-V replied.

Suddenly I had a wonderful thought. 'Mr Chaudhury, what are you going to do with the workshop?' I asked.

Plan Bee

Project *Save the Shop* kicked off properly as soon as we got back to the house.

On the drive from the hills, I'd described Auntie Doré's perfumed candles to Uncle V. He made a whistling-through-his-teeth noise when I told him how much she paid for them. I thought if we could make some out of the local beeswax, and perfume them using the special oils from Mrs Jaffrey's shop in Kochi, then we would have a great all-Indian product for the shop to go with the new fabrics Lula had designed.

Uncle V knew about the problems Lula was having with the business and he also knew how much it meant to her. He said we could use the workshop for some try-outs so long as we could find proper instructions on how to make the candles.

Some of the equipment was still stored in the workshop, but I had no idea how to get from a lump of crumbly beeswax to a beautiful scented candle, and he said he'd rather we didn't burn the workshop down, experimenting.

Uncle V explained we would need to work out the costs of making the candles and getting them over to London, too. Even though he thought it was an interesting idea and said I had a good head for solving problems, he reminded me there was no point unless the candles could make a profit, so I would need to get all the figures ready for Lula to see before I got too excited.

When Priya got back from school that evening I showed her the 'must do' list I had written in the car, and she got started straight away on packaging designs. I gave her the bottle of perfumed oil for inspiration and soon she was tearing pages out of her magazines for mood boards. She decided the perfume was "very natural, but with a spicy twist" and should be packaged in something green with a red accent.

She got her full creative head on and started to explain colour theory to me. It sounded much more scientific than I'd imagined and pretty soon the whole colour wheel thing started spinning too fast, so I left her in order to get on with my own share of the tasks.

While she was busy sketching, I had a long session on the internet researching the 'how to' bit. There was loads online about honey bees and how they were an endangered species in some places. I hadn't realised how important they were to all the other stuff that we eat, not just honey, but everything that needed to be pollinated, like fruit and berries.

I was starting to feel a lot more respectful of bees, and just a bit scared about what was happening to the environment, when I found a beginner's guide to making candles. It didn't look too complicated, but we had to get it right or the candles would spit and smoke, or even fall apart completely.

I printed everything off and highlighted the things we would need, like pans to melt the wax, thermometers, muslin to strain out the bits, cotton for the wicks and something to use as moulds. Then, remembering what Uncle V had said, I started researching how much scented candles sold for in the shops. It was a real eye-popper. Most of them weren't even made of proper beeswax and some of the designer brands were in major double digits for just one candle.

Uncle V had explained that I would need to work the costs out so that after everyone was properly paid we could double the price for the shop. So now, after scrolling through at least a zillion internet pages, I had an idea of the sort of prices we could charge.

Because of where the beeswax came from, we would be able to say our candles were totally organic and that would be a big help. I wondered about adding a bit of information about how important bees were to the environment, when we put the candles on the shelves. Then perhaps people would have an extra reason to buy them.

I went to sleep that night listening to Priya's pencil scratching on her sketch-book. My head was buzzing with ideas about how our candles would help the shop, create new jobs in the village and encourage pollination too. I'd never imagined I had bees to thank for the fruit smoothies I loved.

The next morning, I gave Uncle V the equipment list and he went up to the workshop to see what was still there. I wanted to keep the idea secret until I was sure it would work, so we told Saachi and Lula we were doing a school project, and after a super-fast breakfast we set off for the workshop.

When we arrived, Uncle V was busy fixing up a camping cooker so we would have enough heat to melt the wax down to a liquid ready to strain. I looked at my list, which he had pinned up on the wall. The bit about the budget was highlighted and the word 'profit' had a double red line underneath. It was going to be a very long day.

So much depended on getting the candles right. If this worked, we would have a new product to show Auntie Doré and then she would invest money in the shop to keep it going. If the candles and the new fabric sold quickly, then Lula's money troubles would get better.

Thinking about the consequences, I felt nervous. This was so important to Lula and to our shop, but I'd never done anything like it before. How could I be sure it would work out? As I stared at the list again I realised I couldn't be sure. All I could do was try my hardest, get my friends to help and keep my fingers triple-crossed.

It was a risk, but the pressure was making me feel really energised. This must be how Saachi felt when she got stuck into a new case – no wonder she loved her work.

We went to Granny-ji's for the rest of the stuff we needed. She seemed really excited about the candle project and said it could be 'the start of a new chapter in my life'. She happily emptied her kitchen cupboards and even dug out aprons for us, but we still hadn't found the right thing to use as candle holders. Priya's design needed something natural that would survive the trip to London and wouldn't melt when the candles were lit.

Granny-ji pulled on her apron. It had a picture of Ganesh on the front. I remembered what Uncle V had said about Ganesh helping with new projects.

'Dear Mr Elephant God, we need a bit of inspiration,' I said, putting my hands together and bowing to Granny-ji's belly.

I thought about the day in the forest with Uncle V and the baby elephant splashing in a mud bath, her Mahout using a coconut shell to wash her. 'What about using coconut shells as candle holders!' I said.

'That's brilliant, Cass, and exactly right for my design! They could be wrapped in a palm-leaf bag and tied up with red ribbon.'

It was one problem solved, but now I had to add coconut farming to the list. 'I think we are going to need more help, Priya.'

'But I thought you were the tree-climbing expert around here.'

'Ha-de-ha!' I replied, remembering my first day trip up the wrong banana palm.

'Actually, I know some people who might be able to help,' Granny-ji said. 'Leave it to me.' And she hurried us out of the house.

Once we reached the workshop, Granny-ji took charge. In the time it had taken us to get there, she'd even got busy on the candle-holders and an old man with a machete was standing outside with a bag full of neatly halved coconut shells ready for her to inspect. While she and Priyanka made their selection, I got out the beginner's guide to candles and set up a production line.

The shed was really starting to buzz. Nandita plaited the wicks from multi-coloured threads. They looked great, but they needed coating in wax before we could use them. I cleared a space on the work bench, ran a mini-washing line along the wall and found some scissors.

Granny-ji showed me how to dip the wicks in the

melted wax, cut them to size and hang them to cool on the line. Then I helped Priyanka sieve and strain the wax and pour it into a pan. It would take a few melt-and-sieve sessions before the wax was clean enough to use.

It was very hot in the workshop and every half an hour Uncle V brought in cold drinks. We were all looking a bit crazed. Nandita had a wild smile and bits of wax stuck to her hair, face and clothes. Priya was back stirring the giant melting pot again and muttering like someone doing spells. I could feel twigs sticking out of my hair and I thought there were probably a couple of bees in there too.

Dev had taken charge of the laptop and played us a mix of motivating music. He was also busy with the figures I had scribbled down with the costs and prices from the internet.

During a cold-drink break I looked over his shoulder. Under headings like Postage and Wages, he had columns of numbers set into a table. At the bottom a row was labelled Profit.

'Wow, that looks amazing! How did you do that?'

'It was not so hard. You did all the research, Cassia, I have just organised it. Now, watch this,' he said, pointing to a number at the top of the table. 'This is the price you paid for the beeswax, but of course this price can change. So, if it goes up…' I saw him double the number and press *Enter*.

'The profit figure at the bottom has changed too!' I said.

'It is called a spreadsheet and I think it will be very useful for you.'

'Dev, you're a genius, thank you.' I threw my arms around his shoulders.

'It is certainly very impressive, young man. Are you interested in business as a career choice?' Uncle V had wandered over and was looking at the screen. He changed a couple of the numbers and nodded his head approvingly as the spreadsheet converted them into profit.

By lunchtime we were on the third and final melting and I added a few drops of the perfumed oil to each batch. Then Priyanka poured a little of the molten wax into the shells and I pushed in a length of weighted wick. We wrapped the moulds in banana leaves so they would cool, nice and slowly, then we escaped from the shed and ran down to the sea.

Uncle V and Granny-ji guarded the door of the workshop all afternoon and wouldn't let us in until the sun went down. When we got back from the beach, I was practically hyperventilating with tension. What if the candles hadn't worked? What if we lit one and it just collapsed or, even worse, exploded?

At last, we were all standing in front of the workshop and Uncle V opened the door. The scent of the perfumed oil and beeswax drifted out into the evening sunshine. At the far end of the shed, watched over by Uncle V's little Ganesh figure, the neat row of candles wrapped in their packaging of palm leaves looked perfect. But what would they be like inside? I took a couple of steps forward and then stopped, suddenly unsure about what to do next.

'Go on, London girl, this is it,' Dev said, pointing towards the work bench.

'Yes, Cassia, the moment of truth,' said Granny-ji.

Priya laughed and gave my hand a squeeze. 'I'm sure they will be fantastic, Cassia. You've worked so hard, you really deserve this.'

I felt Nandita's hand on my back, gently pushing me forward and I picked up the nearest package. I untied the cotton. The palm leaves came away from the beeswax easily and the scent of the perfumed oil got even more intense. I set down the candle in its coconut-shell holder on the bench again. Nandita handed me a lighted match. As I held it to the candle, I felt everyone take a deep breath and the match went out.

'Oh purlease! Can you all just chill out before I have a heart attack?' I said.

Nandita had another match ready lit, and this time the candle wick flickered for a moment and then started to burn with a steady flame. We all stood in silence and watched as the candle filled a corner of the room with a golden glow.

Uncle V patted me on the back and said, 'Well done, Cassia, this is a very good show. I am going to fetch Luella and Saachi to see what you young people have done.'

Then he left the workshop to us. Priyanka was studying the packaging for ways to make it better and Nandita was dancing in the shadow of the candle flame. I found Dev's hand and held it tight.

Auntie Doré

While Uncle V was fetching Lula, we lit all the candles and completely filled the workshop with golden light, dancing shadows and the smell of honey, lotus and cinnamon. The old shed looked like a palace from a fairy-story.

Uncle V made Lula close her eyes as she came in. When she opened them she gasped and, as I explained what we had done, I saw she was crying, but in a really happy way. Then she hugged me so tight I thought my ribs would snap.

As soon as we got back from the workshop, Lula locked herself in Saachi's study with Dev's spreadsheet, Priya's drawings, my research and the telephone. Auntie Doré was top of her call list. She also took samples of the more delicate fabrics she had been working on with the new weaving workshop.

Lula had just one chance to stop Auntie Doré heading for the estate agents and putting the shop up for sale. Before she disappeared, Lula asked us loads of questions about the candle-making, and Uncle V and Saachi triple-checked the figures. So it was all up to her now.

'Go for it, Mum,' I whispered, as she closed the study door behind her.

While Lula was phoning Auntie Doré, Priya and Uncle V drove Dev and Nandita home and I sat in the living room with Saachi. I was exhausted, but I couldn't relax until I found out what Auntie Doré thought. I could hear Lula's voice through the walls, but the sounds were too muffled to make out the words. Even though I really hoped it was going well, I felt a bit sad too. If the shop stayed open we would be going home very soon.

Would Uncle V come to London or would he stay in Kerala to get the candle production going? I wouldn't see Priya, Dev, or Nandita again for a long time and when I came back there might be a big hotel on the cliffs and a fenced-off beach.

'Cassia, you should be very proud of what you have achieved today,' Saachi said. 'I just wish the hotel protest was going as well as your candle project!'

'Jonny Gold will be here soon to do the video,' I said.

'Yes, as an aspiring lawyer, what do you think I should say to him?' she asked.

'I'd ask him to build a smaller hotel a little further down the cliff. I'd tell him to leave the mangroves alone and share the beach with the village instead of fencing it off for his guests. He could do loads of good things, if he would just make the development greener and more in harmony with environment,' I replied.

'You are thinking very clearly about this, Cassia, well done. It doesn't seem so very unreasonable to ask a multi-millionaire to share the village with the people who already live here, does it?' she said, shaking her head.

'He could even build a new netball court,' I said, thinking of Nandita and her team. 'Actually, there are a lot of things he could do if he wasn't so selfish and greedy. Do you think he'd listen to us?'

'You mean you and Priyanka?'

'And Dev and Nandita, just like we planned. Maybe we could still do the dance and if he stops to listen, I could talk to him.'

'It's certainly worth a try. Let's decide in the morning exactly what you need to say.'

The headlights of the Green Goddess flashed

across the window and I heard the engine switch off. Priya and Uncle V came in and sat down just as the study door opened and Lula walked into the living room. I studied her face for signs of Auntie Doré's decision, but it was unreadable.

'Well?' said Uncle V.

'Well what?' said Lula.

'Don't you dare torture us!' said Saachi, throwing a cushion across the room at Lula, who ducked just in time.

'Do you mean Doré? Let me try and remember… oh yes… she said… OK! She was very interested in the new fabric range and your candle research intrigued her – it turns out bees are *very* on-trend right now. We have three months to sell enough of the new stock to prove it is worth stocking permanently.'

'Can you do that?' asked Saachi.

'The weavers are all ready and Granny-ji says she can find enough people in the village who remember how the candle workshop used to operate, so we can go into production pretty quickly.'

'That's brilliant news, Mum!'

'It's mostly thanks to you, Cass, you and your lovely new friends. That boy Dev is very handsome, isn't he?'

I froze and Priya started to giggle. I saw Uncle V making arm-waving STOP signs at Lula, but she was being dense and carried on about Dev's friendly eyes and his nice manners. I was glad she liked him and I wanted to tell her the whole story, but not here and not now.

Uncle V had turned into a human windmill, but it was Saachi who rescued me. 'OK, young entrepreneurs, showers and then bed! It's been a long day and you're still covered in bits of candle,' she said, chasing us out of the living room.

I stayed under the shower for ages, feeling the warm water soaking into my hair and loosening the curls. A twig fell from behind my ear and floated towards the plug hole. It was followed by a twist of cotton, and a lump of wax.

While Priya showered, I lay on the bed with my eyes closed, letting the day play back in my head like a film. A few times, I rewound to another secret kiss with Dev in the candlelight and wondered how many more we could share before I went back to London. The shop was safe, for a while at least. Me and Uncle

V had sorted things out and I actually didn't mind if he and Lula got married and we lived in India, for some of the year anyway.

That night I finally finished the Peacock book. In the end, just as the girl in the bookshop said, Una had got into loads of trouble and got dragged home by her dad. She thought being with Ravi would be all lovely and romantic, but it wasn't the happy ending she'd expected and she was going back to England all alone. The whole family thing her dad wanted had crashed out big style, because he didn't see that his girlfriend was a really rubbish stepmum.

I felt sorry for Una. In a way she'd just copied what everyone around her was doing, keeping secrets and telling lies. She only wanted her family to love her, but they'd got all caught up in their own dramas and she'd been pushed away.

It wasn't like that for me. I didn't know how it would work out with Dev, but me and Lula and Uncle V had the bits of a proper happy ending now. There was just one more thing that would make it perfect.

Om Shanti, Babe

A few days later, at *very* stupid o clock, I was woken up by what sounded like a hurricane blasting at the bedroom window. Priya was already out of bed, standing on the balcony and pointing out to sea. Her lips were moving but no sound was reaching into the room. She looked totally crazed, shouting silently with the curtains flapping wildly around her. Clearly, something major was in progress.

I thought about pulling the sheet back over my head and ignoring the dramarama, but then the hurricane noise was joined by someone banging on the bedroom door.

'I really think you should get up, girls. Dev and Nandita are downstairs and I believe a helicopter is trying to land in the garden,' said Lula.

That's when I worked out what Priya was trying to say.

'OMG! He's here! It's today! Jonny Gold Video

Day is now!'

We threw on our dance clothes and ran downstairs. Dev and Nandita were having some breakfast and Priya joined them. I felt sick. How could anyone eat at a time like this?

Saachi came in holding a piece of paper. 'Are you sure you're ready to do this, Cassia?'

'I think so. Anyway, what have we got to lose?'

'Well, there's the beach, the mangroves, the netball court...' She smiled at me and handed over the eco-hotel wish list. It was short, but very clear. I just hoped we could catch Jonny Gold's attention for long enough to get the words out.

As we stepped outside I realised it was going to be a lot harder than I'd imagined. After hovering over the garden and flattening all the plants, the helicopter had landed on the beach and sat surrounded by trucks full of TV cameras and tents packed with costumes and make-up. Everyone was in a hurry, though their main job seemed to be waving clipboards and yelling at one another.

Between the house and the beach a catering truck was setting up and a crush of people waited not very patiently for breakfast. Surrounding the whole area was a fence patrolled by men in uniform with radio phones and don't-even-*think*-about-it expressions.

We walked up to a gap in the fence just as another truck was coming through.

'We've come to see Jonny Gold,' I said.

'Yeah, you and everyone else!' said the driver. His accent sounded like he was from London, too. I wondered if any of the people who'd invaded the beach were local or if they'd all just landed for the day.

'But we need to talk to him.'

'Believe me, today is not the day,' he laughed.

'Please, could you just tell him we're here?'

The driver leaned out of his cab and pointed towards the beach. 'You think I get close enough to his lordship to give him messages? Sorry, kids, forget about meeting Jonny Gold today and just enjoy the sunshine,' he said and he drove away.

I looked to where the driver had pointed. By the water's edge, sitting in an open-sided tent set well apart from the craziness, was Jonny Gold. He was playing his guitar and staring out to sea. A rope barrier around the legs of the tent, and a woman shouting into two mobile phones, seemed to be keeping everyone away. Huge painted screens had been set up on the beach blocking out the view of village houses, so it looked like no one actually lived there.

A track from Jonny Gold's new album was playing through speakers attached to the trunks of the palm trees. As I listened, it changed to *Om Shanti, Babe*, the one Dev had used in the mix on Priya's laptop, the one we had danced to in the workshop. The real Indian-sounding segments were missing of course, but the rhythm was the same.

It should have been a huge chunk of good luck, but we were stuck on the wrong side of the beach with no way across. Saachi was right. The honky-tonk circus had come to town, but we didn't have tickets.

'Cassia, you know how we were going to walk up to Jonny Gold and start dancing...'

I didn't say anything. There wasn't anything I could say. In my head this was supposed to be the easy bit. We were his fans and I thought he'd be pleased to see us. Looking around at all the people and the equipment I realised it was bigger and more complicated than that. Jonny Gold was only a tiny piece in the money-making machine that was set up here and we didn't count at all.

The film set wasn't real in the same way that the village was real. All the cameras would be gone tomorrow and leave nothing behind except Saachi's flattened garden. It was just a big golden bubble. Jonny and his world were inside and we could only sit and watch it float around. I'd wanted to live in a bubble like that once, but I was glad I didn't any more.

'Cass...is there a plan B?' said Priyanka.

'Yeah, we learn to walk on water!' I replied, staring at the sea.

'Actually, we don't need to walk because we have a boat, remember,' she replied.

I looked across at Dev. He was signing to Nandita. She didn't look very happy. I remembered how she had nearly drowned and lost her hearing. No wonder she looked anxious.

Dev took her hand and she followed us round the back of the house to the river. When we reached the boat, Nandita stared at it for a long time and then she stared out at the sea.

I could tell she was trying to make herself step into the boat and I thought she was the bravest person I'd ever met. But she looked as if she was going to be sick and Dev was even worse. He knew how scared his sister was and he also knew how important she was to our plan. He looked torn in two and I thought he was going to stop her, but in the end it was Priyanka who stepped up.

'You can do this without us, Cassia. You and Dev row out and I will stay here with Nandita.'

'But how? What will I do?' I said.

'You'll think of something, London girl,' said Dev, smiling.

We untied the boat and Dev and I dipped the oars into the water and slowly moved away from the riverbank. Priya and Nandita waved sadly as we glided off. I knew they were really disappointed at being left behind and it made me even more determined to talk to Jonny Gold.

Soon we'd left the shelter of the mangroves and were on the open sea. We kept as close to the shore as possible without getting the boat stuck on the sand. The sound from the beach drifted over the waves and I could see Jonny Gold. From a distance, it was like everyone but him was in fast-forward. He was still strumming at his guitar, but now a camera was set up on the sand beside him.

Through the water I could make out the seabed just below us and I felt the boat bump along the bottom, making a scratchy sound as the pebbly sand rubbed on the wood. We both pulled harder on our oars and drifted back into deeper water. Dev didn't say anything, but I saw him smiling encouragingly at me as I hefted the heavy oar out of the water and then dunked it back in.

My hands were starting to hurt and I stopped rowing for a minute to check how close we were to the beach. From over on the sand, I could see the camera operator was pointing at us and waving. Jonny Gold stood up, shielding his eyes against the sun as he looked over towards us.

A motor boat had sped away from the beach and was heading our way. The woman with the mobile phones sat very upright in the passenger seat. She stood up as she got close and I saw her snap the phones closed.

'OK! So here's the deal. Jonny is totally knocked out by you crazy kids, and to say a big *big* thank you for being such fans, he wanted me to give you this.' She leaned forward in the motor boat, flashed a super-white smile, and chucked something towards us. Dev caught it and passed it over to me. It was a signed CD of Jonny Gold's latest album. He'd scribbled *Om Shanti!* on the cover.

'Erm, thanks, but actually we really wanted to talk to him about the hotel.'

The super-white smile disappeared. 'Not possible

today, sweetie,' she said.

I looked over to the beach. Jonny had his back to us. I watched as he threw a cigarette butt on to the sand. He thought we were fans, but he couldn't even be bothered to look at us. In my head, I added up all the money I'd spent on his music and all the hours I'd wasted memorising his lyrics and dreaming about how great he was. They were big numbers for someone who definitely didn't deserve them.

Nandita and Priyanka were standing on the riverbank, waving, and in the distance I could see Saachi's house. Granny-ji, Saachi, Lula and Uncle-V were standing on the balcony. The motor boat was starting to drift away from us. The woman with the phones looked at her watch and bit her lip.

I undid the CD case and slipped Saachi's hotel protest wish-list inside.

'Could you give him this letter, please?' I said and threw the CD back to her. It landed in the bottom of her boat.

'Don't you want the CD?' she said, looking surprised.

'No. No, I don't. This beach doesn't belong to you and Jonny Gold shouldn't build his eco-disaster hotel here,' I said.

The woman looked startled, but she picked up the CD case and then her boat turned away and headed back to the beach.

'I don't know if he will do as you ask, but that was very cool, London girl,' said Dev, doing a little bow. 'And now I think it is time we got ourselves back on to dry land.'

The End (not)

The cabin crew were coming down the aisle, making sure we were all buckled up. My ears popped, and through the window I could see London looming closer. The sky was a solid mass of grey cloud threatening to drop another layer of snow on the buildings below. Goodbye, sunshine, I thought, as I watched the River Thames wiggle away from the city.

Me and Priya had a major weep-fest at the airport, but as soon as we took off I realised I was at the beginning of a new adventure: project Cassia, legal-eagle-eco-girl.

It was going to be a busy year. I had to get a campaign going to save the honey bee and while Priya was in London in the summer, researching fashion colleges, I would be back in Kerala with Saachi, campaigning against the hotel and learning more about the law and the environment.

The shop would be getting a New Year make-over, thanks to Auntie Doré: she'd already started making shelf space for the candles, new fabrics, and even some organic mountain honey.

The big wedding was planned for next Christmas, in the village. It would be good to escape London in winter again. Dad was all excited about travelling somewhere that wasn't actually a war zone and it seemed his new romance was a famous photographer so at least the wedding snaps would be great. I thought it was pretty cool of Lula to invite them both.

I turned away from the window and looked at Lula. Her eyes were closed, but she wasn't asleep. I took hold of her hand and she gave my fingers a squeeze.

'So Cass, my lovely, clever girl, was India as you expected?' she asked, smiling at me.

'No, Mum. It was totally and utterly different and I can't wait to go back!'

The plane rolled to a stop and I reached into my bag for the present Dev had given me. Inside the package was a CD marked "*Om Shanti, Babe* Kerala remix". I smiled, remembering the day in Uncle V's workshop. Just before I left, Nandita had shown me some proper Indian dance moves and I was looking forward to practising them when I got home.

The doors opened and a rush of cold air came into the cabin. It reminded me of setting off on our journey to India. It seemed a very long time ago....

In just a few weeks, a whole world of nicey-spicey-karma-cookie possibilities had shimmied their way into my head. I had lots to look forward to, and yes, everything was going to be all right. Om Shanti.

Om Shanti, BABE

**is the winner of the 2011
Frances Lincoln Diverse Voices
Children's Book Award**

The Frances Lincoln Diverse Voices Children's Book Award was founded jointly by Frances Lincoln Limited and Seven Stories, in memory of Frances Lincoln (1945-2001) to encourage and promote diversity in children's fiction.

The Award is for a manuscript that celebrates cultural diversity in the widest possible sense, either in terms of its story or the ethnic and cultural origins of its author.

The prize of £1500, is awarded to the best work of unpublished fiction for 8-12-year-olds by a writer aged 16 years or over, who has not previously published a novel for children. The winner of the Award is chosen by an independent panel of judges.

Please see the Frances Lincoln or Seven Stories website for further details.

www.franceslincoln.com
www.sevenstories.org.uk